"Are you trying to hide something?" Madelyn asked.

Zach's cheeks warmed with irritation. She was overstepping her boundaries—big-time. "You need to tread carefully, Ms. Sawyer."

"Is that a threat?" Her hands went to her hips.

That text message had done its job, it appeared, because the woman obviously didn't have any faith in him.

"By no means is it a threat. I just think you're not doing yourself any favors storming into town and making accusations."

Flames lit in her eyes just as fireworks began exploding over the water. "Well, maybe you'll believe me now that I really was attacked last night."

He stared back, not one to back down. "I never said I didn't believe you."

"You didn't have to. I could see it in your eyes."

He crossed his arms, growing agitated. "Someone must really not want you here."

"Exactly!"

"But why?" Why would someone feel this threatened by her? That's what didn't make sense. There were obviously things about Madelyn Sawyer that he didn't know yet. "What aren't you telling me?"

They stared at each other another moment. Tension crackled between them.

Christy Barritt's books have won a Daphne du Maurier Award for Excellence in Suspense and Mystery and have been twice nominated for the RT Reviewers' Choice Best Book Award. She's married to her Prince Charming, a man who thinks she's hilarious—but only when she's not trying to be. Christy's a self-proclaimed klutz, an avid music lover and a road trip aficionado. For more information, visit her website at christybarritt.com.

DARK HARBOR

CHRISTY BARRITT

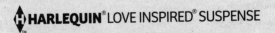
HARLEQUIN® LOVE INSPIRED® SUSPENSE

LOVE INSPIRED BOOKS

ISBN-13: 978-0-373-44749-7

Dark Harbor

Copyright © 2016 by Christy Barritt

This edition published by arrangement with Love Inspired Books.

® and TM are trademarks of Love Inspired Books, used under license. Trademarks indicated with ® are registered in the United States Patent and Trademark Office, the Canadian Intellectual Property Office and in other countries.

www.Harlequin.com

Printed in U.S.A.

Therefore do not worry about tomorrow, for tomorrow will worry about itself. Each day has enough trouble of its own.
–Matthew 6:34

This book is dedicated to all of the fine folks
over on the Eastern Shore of Virginia.
I've truly enjoyed getting to know you all as I've been
researching the area for the past several months.

ONE

Madelyn Sawyer glanced into her rearview mirror again and her pulse spiked. The white truck with the dent in its front bumper was still there. Still following her.

She drew in an uneven breath as she dragged her eyes back to the highway in front of her. The road ahead was fairly empty aside from a tractor trailer that had passed her a few minutes earlier and an old school bus full of migrant workers that had just pulled onto the street.

Madelyn was still ten minutes away from her end destination: the small bay town of Waterman's Reach. Would the truck follow her all the way there?

As the sun continued to sink lower on the horizon, her thoughts raced. Was someone trying to scare her, keep tabs on her or harm her? None of the options made her feel better.

There was already enough secrecy surrounding her assignment in the small fishing community. The last thing she needed was to draw unnecessary attention to herself. Apparently, she already had.

She glanced in the mirror again. Each glimpse of the truck ratcheted up her nerves. What was she going to do?

The truck had been behind her for the past twenty miles. Madelyn had tried to blow it off by rationalizing that many people traveled this route straight from Maryland all the way to Norfolk, Virginia. The region, known as the Eastern Shore, was a strip of land, a peninsula that was surrounded by the ocean on one side and the Chesapeake Bay on the other.

She'd gotten off the highway twice to test the truck. The vehicle may have disappeared for short periods, but it always appeared again behind her. She didn't know what was going on or why someone would follow her.

But she had to end this. Now.

With her grip tight on the steering wheel, she swerved onto a side street. She hoped her GPS would reroute her to the duplex where she was staying and that being on a secluded road with the truck wouldn't lead to more danger. Losing the truck was all she could think of.

Unfortunately, she'd been trained as a journalist and not in defensive or evasive driving techniques. Maybe she should add those to her bucket list. At times like this it would come in handy.

Though the speed limit was only thirty-five, she gunned the engine of her eight-year-old sedan. The Nissan wasn't what it used to be, and her motor groaned as she accelerated.

She didn't care. She'd worry about her car later. Right now she wanted to get away and lose this truck once and for all. She feared her very life might depend on it.

The road was narrow with deep ditches on either side. Maybe pulling off hadn't been the greatest of ideas. Her location allowed little room for error. She became more secluded with every rotation of the tires.

Madelyn glanced in the rearview mirror again. The truck had turned after her!

Her heart rate ratcheted again. What was she going to do? None of this made sense.

Only one person knew her real reason for coming here—her editor. Paula would have no reason to expose Madelyn's true intentions—it would cost them the story of a lifetime if she did. Something was seriously wrong.

A half a mile later she swerved into a gravel lane and gunned it, traveling down the street as quickly as possible. She had to lose the truck. As she pulled into a service road ending in the woods, she heard a pop. Her car bounced and bumped.

She'd busted a tire, she realized.

Great.

She'd have to address that in a moment. For now, she cut her car lights, hoping she'd remain concealed in the shadows.

Her heart pounded in her ears as she waited. Would the truck follow her? Trap her here?

If that happened, what would the driver do to her? Did he want to hurt her?

None of this made sense.

She continued to wait, her heart pounding out of control. She imagined the pain she might endure if the wrong person found her. Torture. Suffering. Who knew what else?

Each thought caused her anxiety to skyrocket even more.

As perspiration sprinkled her forehead, she glanced at the time. It had been five minutes and no truck. Could she really have lost him? It seemed too good to be true.

She sucked on her bottom lip a moment, still trying to figure out why she would be followed. There was only one person who wouldn't want her to write the article, and that was the town's police chief, Zach Davis. But even he didn't know she was coming or what her real motivation was.

As far as everyone else knew, she was writing a travel article on the quaint town. Its location between the Chesapeake Bay and the Atlantic Ocean made it an ideal spot for the flourishing seafood industry.

Madelyn wasn't here for the fishing, though. She didn't

even like to eat seafood, truth be told. But she *was* here to fish for what could be the story of her life.

Being here was precarious. Her assignment involved a trace amount of deceit. But the rewards outweighed the risks. At least, that's what she told herself. Her conscience kept contradicting the thought.

She justified her actions with one word: *justice.* She could expose wrongs done by the arrogant and help them to get the negative exposure they deserved. It was what every good journalist wanted—to be a voice of change and reason. To make a difference. To impact the world.

She held her breath as a shadow overtook the mouth of the service road. Another vehicle was coming toward her, she realized.

Her blood spiked with adrenaline. She needed a weapon, a way to protect herself. But she had nothing. And she'd secluded herself in the middle of the woods where no one would hear her scream.

Her cell phone, she realized. She could call for help! Except when Madelyn turned it on, her screen showed she had no reception.

Before she could second-guess herself, Madelyn climbed from the car, grabbed her purse and darted into the woods. She ran as hard as she could, her ankles twisting in her heels. She couldn't be sure how far she'd gotten. But when she saw the car pull up behind hers, she froze, ducking behind a tree. She couldn't risk being spotted.

Peering out, she watched carefully as the vehicle came to a stop behind hers, essentially blocking her in. Only, it wasn't the white truck. It was a police cruiser.

She sucked in a quick breath.

A police cruiser?

Dread filled her when she saw the man who'd stepped out. Zach Davis. She'd recognize him anywhere thanks to all of the research she'd done on the man. Just because he was knock-me-over gorgeous with his curly blond hair and blue eyes didn't mean he was a good guy.

Was he trying to stop Madelyn before she got to town and uncovered all of the unsavory moments of his life?

Was he somehow working with the driver of that white truck? It was the only thing that made sense. He must have somehow found out Madelyn was coming and planned his defense. All of her assumptions about the man were proving to be true. He deserved to be locked behind bars.

He marched toward her car and peered inside.

Madelyn made sure not to move, to remain perfectly still.

As the police chief straightened, his gaze skimmed the area.

Madelyn held her breath. Would he see her? For her safety, she prayed he didn't. Because if he was as dangerous as she thought, she was in real trouble.

Zach Davis sensed he was being watched. As he scanned the woods, his gaze tried to zero in on something out of place. Proof teased the edge of awareness. Something was there. Hidden yet possible to find.

His hand went to his gun, just to be safe.

He'd gotten a report of a car driving erratically in this area. Since he was already close by, he'd decided to check it out. He'd followed the trail of dust on the gravel lane and found the burgundy Nissan. Where had the driver gone?

He'd already recorded the license plate number, and the car's make and model. He'd run them soon. Until then, he had to pinpoint why he felt like he was being watched.

"I know you're there. Come out." His hand remained on his gun. "Let's make this easy on both of us."

A squirrel scattered up a tree. A bird chirped as it hurried across the canopy of branches overhead. A fly buzzed at his ear.

But silence was the only response from the person hiding. Usually people only hid when they were guilty of something. What was this person up to?

"Don't make this harder than it has to be," he continued. He shifted, trying to get a better look. He saw a gleam as sunlight hit something reflective. Sunglasses maybe?

A woman, he realized.

"I'm Police Chief Zach Davis from Waterman's Reach. I won't hurt you. We just need to talk."

Again, nothing.

He stepped closer, afraid he would scare the woman and she'd take off in a run. She'd get lost in these woods. There were miles and miles of them out here. If the woods didn't get to her, the wild animals would. Cottonmouths had been especially rampant this year.

"I have all of the time in the world," he continued. "You can try to wait me out, but it won't work. You can run, but you're going to put yourself at risk of getting lost, getting injured or being dinner for some of the wildlife out here. It's your choice. I'd say I'm the least scary of all of them."

That seemed to do the trick. The woman stepped out ever so slightly, her hands in the air and an untrusting look in her eyes. "I assure you, I'm not looking for trouble."

"Then why are you running?"

"Why are you chasing me?" she countered.

"Chasing you? I'm just following the lead of a citizen who was concerned by careless driving."

"I was only driving carelessly because someone was following me."

Following her? Was he dealing with someone who struggled with paranoia? Or was someone actually following the woman?

"Why don't you step out here so we can talk like two rational human beings?" he asked.

"How do I know I can trust you?" Her voice wavered.

"I'm a cop. I have no reason to hurt you. Unless you're aiming a gun at me, we should be just fine."

Finally the woman emerged from the woods, wobbly in her high heels. Her gray skirt was stained and there was a leaf in her hair.

His breath caught for a moment.

She definitely didn't look like she was from around here. Her hair was brown and glossy and cut neatly to her shoulders. She wore a white top with black polka dots and a straight gray skirt that reached her knees. Her heels looked uncomfortably high, and her purse probably cost more than Zach made in one week.

Both her words and the way she spoke indicated she was well educated. Just who was she, though? She just didn't fit into the dynamic he'd experienced so far in the town. Most people here were grounded in the fishing industry. They had deep tans, easy accents and chose jeans to pencil skirts.

Most people who came into town for work had something to do with the seafood industry. But this woman did not appear to be the type to deal with fish or oysters. She looked too big-city.

Despite his initial attraction, his next thought quickly dampened the surge. She reminded him of Julia, he realized, the woman who'd broken his heart after the Baltimore fiasco when she'd left him faster than someone fleeing an oncoming tornado.

"A white truck followed me on my way down from Maryland," the woman started. "I pulled off the main road trying to get away from it. I thought you could be connected with the other driver."

She sounded scared but otherwise rational.

Concern filled him. If she was telling the truth—and he was beginning to think she was—then this could be a bad situation. "Any idea why someone might be following you?"

"None." She crossed her arms.

"An ex-boyfriend?"

She shook her head. "No. Not a current boyfriend or spouse either. I have no good ideas as to whom this might be."

"What's your name, ma'am?"

She licked her lips, looking almost reluctant. "Madelyn Sawyer."

"Where are you headed, Madelyn?"

Her frown deepened. "Waterman's Reach."

His eyebrows shot up. The town didn't have that many visitors. City council wished they did. They pushed to have more people. But especially this time of the year, the place was mostly locals—5,479 to be exact. As the new chief, he made sure he knew all he could about the town.

"What brings you there?"

Her chin jutted up. "I'm writing an article, if you must know. A travel article. I've already been in touch with Eva Rogers, and she's expecting me."

He shifted, finally moving his hand from his gun. He had received some kind of memo about a visit from a reporter. The mayor had encouraged city employees to make her feel welcome and had reminded them how important this push for tourism was.

Zach had essentially ignored the memo. He'd had no intention of interacting with the reporter. No, a reporter was the last person he wanted to have contact with. He didn't need some nosy journalist digging into his background. If she did, his whole investigation could be ruined.

"Do you remember anything about this truck that was following you?" he asked, suddenly ready to have this conversation done.

"Not much. It was white, probably ten years old, with tinted windows and a dent in the front bumper. Sound familiar?" Was that a challenge in her voice? What sense did that make?

"Can't say it does. But I'll see what I can find out."

"I'd appreciate it." She stared at her flat tire.

"Do you have a spare?" Zach asked. As much as he'd like to limit their interaction, that wasn't going to be possible, was it?

She shook her head. "The last time I had a flat, my spare popped. I've had a bit of bad luck when it comes to car problems lately."

"I can give you a ride back." It was the least he could do. If there was some kind of threat on this woman's life, he needed to do his duty as police chief. Then he wanted to be done with her.

He paused before climbing into his cruiser. A branch snapped in the woods. It wasn't an unusual sound in itself. It could be a deer or even a raccoon. But that familiar feeling of being watched filled him again.

He glanced around but saw no one. What if Madelyn was telling the truth? What if the driver of that white truck was out in those woods somewhere watching them?

He scanned the woods one more time.

Then he heard the sound of someone crashing through the underbrush.

"Stay here!" he shouted before darting into the forest.

TWO

Zach dodged trees and stumps and underbrush as he rushed after the figure in the distance. The woods were thick and hard to navigate. But he needed to figure out who was out there.

Maybe the person fleeing was a hunter who'd stumbled across them and feared getting caught without a permit. It was a possibility. And some hunters would run rather than face fines.

Zach reached a slight clearing and paused. He'd lost sight of the man he was following. Where had he gone?

He listened, hoping for a clue. Nothing signaled the man's location. Cautiously, he took a step forward. He surveyed the area, his instincts on alert.

The man couldn't have just disappeared. Was he hiding? Waiting to ambush Zach?

He had to be careful. He'd seen firsthand just how easy it was for an officer of the law to lose his life. Too many good people had died in the line of duty.

As he took another step toward an especially thick section of trees, he heard something click.

A gun, he realized.

Zach ducked to the ground. His heart pounded in his ears. He listened for footsteps, for any sign the gunman was getting closer or trying to stage an ambush.

Nothing.

Then a crack filled the air.

Something whizzed over him and splinters rained on his shoulders.

A bullet had hit the tree above him, he realized. A few more inches, and he would have been toast.

Heavy footsteps darted away. Branches snapped. Underbrush rustled.

Zach sprang to his feet, darting toward the sound. The man busted through the woods. Zach caught a glimpse of a long-sleeved black shirt, black pants and a black hat. Whoever was out here wasn't a hunter. But he was trying to remain concealed. That was the only reason someone dressed like that.

Zach thrust himself through the wilderness, trying to reach the man. Shooting at a police officer was a serious crime. Zach had to do everything he could to catch the man.

A clearing stretched ahead. This was his chance.

Zach pushed himself harder.

A whistle sounded in the distance. He glanced over and saw a train traveling toward them down the tracks. His breath caught.

No…

With a burst of energy, he sprinted toward the man, gaining speed by the moment.

Just as the man crested the tracks, the train barreled past.

Zach stepped back as the force of the engine brought with it a rush of wind. His hands went to his hips and he shook his head.

The shooter's timing had been impeccable. Two more minutes' difference would have yielded different results. Zach could have caught him, pulled that mask off and figured out who the man was, once and for all.

Zach stared down the length of the train—it was long.

Really long. He knew by the time it went past, the man would be gone.

Shaking his head, Zach stomped back toward the sight of the shooting. He found the bullet lodged into the tree and studied it for a moment. He couldn't tell much about it. He only knew it had come way too close to his head.

He pulled some tweezers and a bag from his pocket and collected the bullet. He used his phone to take some pictures.

He searched the ground for footprints, but they'd had a dry summer and the soil was rock hard. Just as he suspected, he found nothing.

He gave one last glance in the direction the bullet had come from and then turned back.

He had to make sure Madelyn Sawyer was okay. Because he had a feeling this all led back to her.

Madelyn felt beside herself. She'd been followed, stranded in the middle of nowhere and then she'd heard a gunshot. Had the chief been injured? Or had Zach Davis shot someone? Who had that man in the woods been?

The questions all collided in her mind.

She heard someone moving through the woods and froze.

Was it Zach? Or could it be the driver of the white truck? Her nerves were getting the best of her and making it hard to breathe.

In the quiet moments by herself, she'd remembered the truck. She'd remembered the risks she was taking by coming here. This could be her big break, she reminded herself. If she was able to get some dirt on Zach Davis, it could be the story of her life. The story that would make her boss proud. That would cement her role in the world of respected journalists who'd written stories that made a difference.

She backed away from the tree line, putting her car between her and whoever was coming her way. This was how it all ended in scary movies. A woman alone in the woods, thinking help was coming when it was really the killer.

She swallowed hard and glanced around for something to protect herself with. All she saw was gravel and sticks.

It was going to have to work.

She reached down and scooped up some pebbles. She could use them to distract someone, if it came down to it.

She crouched behind the car, waiting, anticipating.

Finally, a figure broke through the trees. Her eyes were riveted on the man.

Zach, she realized as his features came into focus. It was Zach. Her shoulders slumped with relief.

He lumbered onto the service road and squinted when he saw her behind the car.

"Are you okay?" he asked.

She stood, dropping the pebbles and straightening her outfit. She raised her chin as she looked at him. "I'm fine. I heard a gun…"

"Someone shot at me."

Her pulse spiked. This was worse than she imagined. "Did you catch him?"

Zach shook his head. "No. He got away, thanks to a train passing through. But I have the bullet and I plan to run ballistics on it."

"I'm glad…you're okay." Where had that come from? Zach Davis was possibly a bad cop, someone who deserved to be locked up. She shouldn't be wishing the best for him.

"I can only assume it was a hunter trying to scare me away. I can't think of any other explanation. Can you?" He challenged her with his gaze.

Her cheeks heated, and she shook her head. *Great. He already suspects me.* "I still have no idea why I was followed."

His accusatory gaze remained on her another moment

before he finally looked away. "I guess we should get you into town, so I can get back to the office and process this."

She swallowed hard. "That sounds like a great idea."

Zach grabbed her suitcase and placed it in the trunk before they both climbed into his police cruiser. The car was neat with a leathery scent. Madelyn tried to settle back into the vehicle and not give any signals that she knew who Zach Davis really was. But it was hard to hide her nervous energy. She wanted to tap her foot, to play with her hair, to do uncountable things that could clue Zach in that she was on edge.

"Sorry about your arrival in town." Zach headed back down the service road, his arm slung across the seat as he peered out the back glass.

"These things happen, I suppose. Just not usually to me."

He offered an apologetic smile and pulled out onto the side street. "So, you're writing a tourism piece?"

Madelyn nodded, realizing he was just making polite conversation. She had to chill out if she didn't want to raise suspicions. "That's right. I'm with East Coast International. You ever heard of it?"

"Sounds vaguely familiar. I don't read too many regional magazines, however." He glanced at her as the miles began to blur past. "Have you written a lot of travel articles?"

"I've done my fair share." It was almost all she'd done, truth be told. But she longed for more. To do articles that made a difference. She wanted to be a voice of change, someone who could help the helpless, who brought justice to those who deserved it.

They were lofty goals. But she held tight to them.

"Why Waterman's Reach?" Zach asked.

She shrugged, trying to remain calm. "The town seemed like an undiscovered treasure. That's what I like. Anyone can write about Myrtle Beach or Williamsburg or the popular tourist spots. I want to show the places off the beaten path."

"Well, you've definitely got the undiscovered part down being in Waterman's Reach."

She glanced at him. It was hard for her to comprehend that the very man she'd done so much research on was here now. She was riding with him. Close enough to touch. A hint of thrill, as well as fear, spread through her.

She cleared her throat. "How about you? How long have you been here?"

Was it her imagination or did Zach's gaze darken at her question?

"A few months." He didn't offer any more details.

"So you're not a local." She tried to sound surprised. "I always imagined a town like Waterman's Reach to be the kind where jobs like police chief were handed down generationally."

He smiled softly, maybe sadly. "No, I'm an outsider, which has brought some challenges of its own. In fact, the prior police chief's nephew works under me. But the mayor thought some change would be good for the town."

"Has it been?" she asked.

"You'll have to ask the people in town that question." Just as he said that, he turned off the main highway and into Waterman's Reach. A quaint-looking town came into view. She quickly glimpsed the cobblestone sidewalks, antique-looking streetlights and picturesque storefronts.

Before she could soak too much of it in, Madelyn looked down at the paper where she'd jotted her travel information and rattled off the address. Zach turned off Main Street and pulled to a stop in a parking lot behind the downtown area in Waterman's Reach.

"This is where you're going?" Zach looked around as if confused. There were no bed-and-breakfasts or hotels close, which might explain why he looked baffled.

She pointed to a house across the lot. "Right there, if I understand correctly."

Thank goodness she'd taken the time to look up the address online, so she had some idea of how the duplex looked. Dusk had fallen now, casting dim shadows on everything. She'd wanted to get here while it was still daylight outside, but that plan had been interrupted.

"Mayor Ron Alan's rental property?" Zach asked.

"Yes, that's correct. He's letting me use it while I'm in town." She still felt a little guilty about it. The mayor had gone out of his way to make her feel welcome. How would he feel when he found out she wasn't writing a travel article but instead a hit piece on the town's police chief?

"Mayor Alan owns quite a bit of real estate in the area," Zach told her. "That's how he originally made a name for himself. He used his inheritance to buy up real estate when the prices were low, and now he rents them out. In fact, even my house belongs to the man."

"Small-town dynamics, huh? You've got to love them."

He put the car in Park and started to get out.

"I can get my suitcase. Don't worry about it," Madelyn insisted.

He paused, one leg already on the ground. "I don't mind. I can walk it up for you."

"No, really. I've already put you out today, and I know you have reports to file, especially since that bullet came your way. Let me handle my suitcase." She really wanted to be away from the man. She needed space to collect her thoughts.

"If you insist." He shrugged, closing his door again. "If you have any more problems while you're in town, let me know. In the meantime, I'll call a tow truck to pick up your car. Fisher's Auto Repair is the closest. Next shop is about thirty minutes out."

"Fisher's will be fine."

"Will do."

Her hands trembled as she stepped from the car and onto the cracked asphalt of the small, shadowed parking lot. Zach popped the trunk, and she ran around to grab her suitcase. Handle in hand, she leaned into the car once more. "Thanks again."

"Hope you get that article written without any trouble," he said.

His words froze her a moment. Then she realized it wasn't a threat, but an observation based on what had happened earlier today.

She let out an airy laugh. *Not a smooth move, Madelyn. You've got to be on the ball here.*

"Thank you," she murmured. She waved and took a step back.

"I'll wait until you get inside."

"I'll be fine. I want to stretch my legs for a moment." She needed to be away from his scrutiny as soon as possible.

He raised his eyebrows, as if he doubted her words. "As you wish."

She waited until he pulled away to survey the area for any sign of danger, hating how her body had gone into fight-or-flight mode. All she spotted was the back side of the shops lining Main Street. A municipal lot was located dead center between buildings and houses that formed a U around it.

That U shape also meant she was hidden from eyesight from anyone walking the town's sidewalks. The area back here was deserted, as most of the businesses had already closed for the evening.

The good news was that she didn't see the white truck anywhere.

The bad news was that, if the truck's driver did show up, no one would be around to hear her scream.

She shivered at the thought. All the craziness from earlier had shaken her up. Being followed. Meeting Zach the way she had. Hearing he'd been shot at.

It would leave anyone unsettled.

She glanced up at the house in front of her. Her temporary home was a two-level duplex the mayor owned and used as rental property. The home looked contemporary, well kept and clean with its blue siding and white trim. She was staying on the second floor, and if she understood correctly, the first floor was currently unoccupied.

She approached the stoop. A cardboard box had been left there with her name on it. Cautiously, she took the note on top off.

"For Madelyn, welcome to Waterman's Reach. Here are some of our famous oysters to give you a taste of the town. Cordially, Mayor Alan."

Madelyn swallowed a bitter taste in her mouth.

Instead of dwelling on her deceit now, she glanced around. Where was that lockbox where she could get the key?

By the garage, she remembered. She walked to the small building at the side of the house, found a small case beside the electrical box and turned the numbers there until the code was entered. The mechanism clicked open, and she pulled the key out.

As she walked back toward the door, she shuddered. There was something about being alone in a new place that always got to her. She tried to be tough. But on the inside, she constantly battled herself and her fears.

It wasn't a fun position to be in.

She was going to get through this and prove to her colleagues that she was someone to watch out for in the field of investigative journalism.

She wanted to—no, make that *needed* to—prove herself.

The realization seemed a bit pitiful. She shouldn't have to prove herself. But something was programmed into her thoughts, something at gut level, that made her believe that her self-worth was based on a certain set of criteria, no matter how much she might deny it.

She paused when she heard a sound behind her. Her shoulders instantly tightened. What was that?

She turned but saw nothing. Just trash cans, some old pallets and a broom.

Strange.

With a touch of hesitation, Madelyn hurried toward the door, her heels clacking against the pavement. That was rule number one that her mentor had taught her: always dress for success.

Madelyn heard that sound behind her again and paused. Fear began to gel in her stomach. Before she could turn, a hand covered her mouth.

Her heart surged with panic. What was happening?

Was she being robbed? Mugged? Murdered?

"Get out of this town," someone whispered in her ear.

THREE

Madelyn froze as she waited for the man's next threat, his next demand. Waited for the pain she was about to experience.

"You shouldn't have ever come here." His voice sounded gruff, commanding.

His gloved hand pressed hard into her mouth. Hard enough that her teeth ached, that they cut into her gums and lips. His arm locked her in place. The man was strong, and his hold was like a clamp.

Madelyn's gaze darted around. There was no one around to help her. To see the act happening. To report to the police that she was missing.

Her heart ached at the thought. There'd be no one to mourn her. She was alone in this world, and never had she remembered that fact like she did now.

"Go back to Maryland," the man continued. "Understand?"

She didn't dare speak.

"Understand?" He squeezed her until she yelped.

She nodded, desperate for her life.

She wanted to fight, but she was frozen. Did he have a knife? A gun? Would he kill her?

Instead, his hand slipped. In one slick movement, he

shoved her to the ground. Quickly, he reached down and grabbed the oysters. Then he fled.

She looked over her shoulder in time to spot a figure dressed in black. She couldn't tell anything else about him. He was too much of a blur, a shadow, as he bolted away.

She sank to the ground, her knees going weak. Her insides were a quivering mess. Her whole life had flashed before her eyes, and she'd feared the worst. She'd feared she would join her parents.

Only—would she? They'd believed in God and in Heaven. Madelyn certainly didn't believe in God anymore, and she wasn't sure what she thought about Heaven or life after death.

She only knew there was a massive hole in her heart after her parents—her only family, since she had no siblings—had been stripped from her.

All she'd lived for since their death was her career. It seemed like the only sure thing about her future—at least it was her best hope. She couldn't let some bully pressure her into giving up her dreams and goals.

She sucked in a deep breath, trying to compose herself and not fall apart.

With another shudder of fear, she hurried back to her suitcase, picked it up and went to the house. Her hands trembled as she tried to put the key in the lock.

She just wanted to be somewhere safe.

Did someone know who she was? Know why she was really here? What else might he do to ensure she actually *did* go home?

The only person who may feel threatened by Madelyn was Zach. She shook her head. He shouldn't have any clue who she really was. Paula was the only one who knew her true motives for coming here.

That's when Madelyn realized the truth: she needed to report a crime.

It looked like she and Zach Davis were going to have to talk again. Maybe this was a good thing. After all, what better way to track down the truth than by getting to know him more?

Zach leaned back in the ratty old desk chair and thought about what had happened earlier. All of it seemed out of the realm of the ordinary for the quiet town.

If Madelyn was telling the truth—and he had no reason to suspect she wasn't—she'd been followed into town. Then someone had shot at Zach. What an utterly strange greeting for the town's visitor.

The town's very intriguing visitor. Yet, her gaze had been shifty and her actions showed anxiety. Was she hiding something? Or was she simply shaken up after everything that had happened?

He surveyed his small, quiet office. He had a secretary/receptionist/dispatcher and one officer here in the fishing community. He could use more help, but the mayor had yet to approve the budget increase.

Zach had only been in Waterman's Reach for three months—barely enough time to learn the ropes and fully comprehend how the small department here operated. So far, he knew the town was sleepy.

He'd been inching closer and closer to this exact location and this exact job. As soon as he heard about the position opening up, he jumped on the opportunity to come here.

He'd done his homework. He knew that Waterman's Reach was the most likely spot where he'd find answers about the crime that haunted him. Gone was the big-city excitement of being a detective. His work in Baltimore had never been done—he didn't have enough hours in his day to give the attention needed to each one of his cases. Here, he experienced a slower pace of life.

He actually kind of liked the change. What he didn't like

was the lives that had been affected by what had happened in Baltimore before he left. The families that had been hurt. The futures that had been destroyed.

He crushed the paper cup in his hand and tossed it into the trash can. With any luck, he would find some answers here and be able to move on with his life eventually. The only caveat was that he had to ensure that no one could figure out who he really was in the meantime. If they did, his whole investigation—years of work—would be ruined.

He felt the air in the building change as the front door opened, and he waited for Lynn to greet the visitor. When he didn't hear anything, he stood and stretched his taut muscles before stepping out of his office. Now where had Lynn gone? Her desk was empty.

"Can I help—?" He stopped abruptly when he saw the familiar figure. "Madelyn. What brings you by here? I called the tow truck, but I'd give Fisher's a little bit longer—"

"It's not about my car. It's about the man who just attacked me."

He bristled. Attacked? On the surface, violence didn't seem to exist in Waterman's Reach.

Until Madelyn Sawyer showed up.

"Attacked you?" he repeated.

She nodded, lowering her gaze for a minute. Her hand went to the counter as if she needed to steady herself. Just then he noticed her bloody knee and the rip in her skirt.

"Do you need to sit down?" he asked. "Go to the hospital?"

She offered what was probably supposed to be a reassuring smile. "I'll be fine. Thank you."

His curiosity continued to grow. "Could you tell me what happened?"

"A man came up behind me, put his hand over my mouth and demanded that I leave town. Then he stole my…" She frowned. "Oysters."

His concern temporarily disappeared as she finished her sentence. Certainly he hadn't heard her correctly. "Oysters?"

Her frown deepened. "I knew I shouldn't have mentioned that part."

"Why don't you come into my office and I'll take your statement?"

"I'd appreciate that." She took a few steps toward Zach as he extended his hand toward the open door in the distance.

Just as she reached him, her knees gave out. Zach grabbed her elbow to steady her. As he did, electricity shot through him.

He quickly pulled himself together and tried to forget the scent of lilac perfume that had wafted up toward him. She held her head up higher, surprisingly tense. She was probably shaken after what just happened. No one could blame her for that.

He pulled out a padded seat across from his desk.

"Please." He waited until she was seated before walking to the other side and lowering himself into the beat-up swivel chair he'd inherited from the previous chief. Levi Watson had cared more about giving himself bonuses than he had for building upgrades or equipment updates. "Now, please tell me exactly what happened."

She ran through her story.

"He actually reached down and took the oysters before he left?" He had to ask the question because that aspect of the crime seemed so obscure.

Madelyn scowled, as if she didn't appreciate him following up. "That's correct."

As he shifted in his seat, the chair squealed beneath him. "Did you get a look at him?"

"I only saw that he was wearing black."

All black? Could it be the same person who'd shot at him in the woods? His instincts said yes.

Something in her gaze caused his guard to rise. Was she hiding something? But what? If that was the case, certainly she could have come up with a better cover story than stolen oysters.

"I never asked you earlier: how long will you be in town?" Zach asked.

"At least a week."

He contemplated her answer a moment before nodding. Her explanation seemed reasonable enough. "I'll see what I can find out. I have to admit, what you've told me isn't much to go on, but I will check with some of the shop owners with businesses near the duplex and find out if they saw anything suspicious."

"I don't really want to draw any attention to myself." She shrugged, as if her words might have sounded strange. "It's only smart as a single woman."

"I'll use caution."

She nodded as she stood, clutching her purse. "I appreciate that. Thank you."

"I'll be in touch, Ms. Sawyer." As he watched her retreat, something felt unsettled in his gut.

There was something she wasn't telling him. Now he just had to figure out what and why.

Zach followed her out into the reception area. Lynn had returned, a steaming microwave meal in front of her and an apologetic smile on her face. He nodded at her as he stepped outside the small office building located on the edge of the town's retail area.

He let his gaze wander down the sidewalk. He expected to see Madelyn. Instead, his attention was drawn to his police cruiser. The tires were all flat.

He bent down to examine them and saw slashes in the thick rubber. Someone had done that on purpose. But what kind of message were they trying to send? That he wasn't welcome here?

Some didn't approve of an outsider being chief. Since he'd arrived in town, his mailbox had been knocked over. Some potted plants on his deck had been smashed. A dead fish had been left outside his window at the police station. Now this.

Did that mean that someone knew about his past? The thought made him bristle.

If someone knew who he was, that could sabotage his whole investigation—which was his entire reason for being here.

He couldn't let that happen.

"I'm not sure I can do this," Madelyn mumbled into the phone.

She paced the kitchen floor while dark windows stared at her in the distance. As unexplainable nerves got the best of her, she pulled her sweatshirt closer around her, wishing for a moment she was back in her safe little apartment in Maryland. At least she had a few neighbors there who would notice if something was wrong or that she could run to if she had any trouble. Here, she felt alone and out of place. She kept reliving her earlier encounter outside the house.

"Madelyn, of course you can do this," her editor, Paula, said. "This will be your big story, the one that propels you to the top. You can't back out now."

"But I talked to Zach. He didn't seem evil or murderous or like a bad cop even." He'd been quite handsome, truth be told. And kind. He didn't look cold-blooded, not even when he'd pushed Madelyn for more answers than she'd wanted to give.

"You could tell what was going on deep inside of the man after talking to him twice? People often hide who they really are, Madelyn. You can't take everyone at face value, and if you're going to make it as a journalist, you're going to have to finely tune your reporting instincts. No more thinking with your heart. None of this misplaced compassion. You're good at getting people to trust you. Get Zach to trust you also."

Madelyn frowned and leaned against the wall a moment, staring at the dark beach beyond her window. She couldn't make anything out except an occasional whitecap hitting the sand.

Seeing the bay made her feel small and reminded her what a big world it was out there. Since her parents had died, she'd felt all alone without any kind of support system to fall back on.

Her mom and dad had gone out to dinner one night and neither had come home. They'd been in a car wreck. A police officer had been in pursuit of a suspect after a bank robbery. He'd gone through an intersection and rammed into her parents' car, killing them on impact.

The officer hadn't lost his job, and his apology hadn't meant anything considering the loss Madelyn had faced.

She had been only eighteen at the time. Her childhood had ended on that day, never to be regained.

A few months later she'd gone off to college and tried to forge a new life for herself. Paula had been a graduate assistant for one of her professors and had seen promise in one of Madelyn's essays. She'd given her guidance when Madelyn had no one else.

After college, Paula began working at East Coast International Magazine. Five years later she became editor. Paula had hired Madelyn last year after she'd gained some experience by working for a few small-town newspapers in the years after college.

Paula was everything Madelyn wanted to be. She was smart, successful and respected. But their personalities were quite different. Like night and day for that matter. Paula was brash, bold and said what was on her mind. Madelyn, on the other hand, was softer, kinder and more contemplative.

She snapped back to the conversation. *Get Zach to trust you*, Paula had said.

This was going to require a certain level of deceit on Madelyn's part. She'd thought about this a lot before she'd come. Could she really handle the task? Earlier, she thought she could. But now she was beginning to doubt herself and her reasons for being here.

"You're sure Zach is guilty?"

"Madelyn, it's his fault that two police officers died, not to mention that poor boy."

"That poor boy was a drug dealer," Madelyn reminded her. "Not that he should have been shot. But he was about to shoot Zach."

"Rumor has it that Zach Davis was involved in the drug ring, and that's why those two officers were killed. It was no mistake. People think that Zach didn't want to be caught and that something went down during the bust that might indicate his guilt and involvement in the whole thing."

"That's going to be difficult to prove." Why had Paula sent her here to do this job? She claimed it was because she was editor now and that she was trying to give Madelyn the break she wanted. But Paula was the type who liked to do things herself. The question had wafted through Madelyn's mind more than once.

"Zach can be quite charming. That's what I heard at least. Don't fall under his spell."

Madelyn straightened. "Wait—did you know him?" Was there more to Paula's determination to see this article through than she'd originally let on?

"No, of course not. I just know people who know him. He's a horrible person masquerading as someone who's noble. He needs justice, Madelyn, and you're the one who's going to give it to him. Can I count on you?"

Madelyn wished she felt so certain. That pesky compassion always crept in at the worst times and sometimes made her wonder if she was suited for this career. She wasn't cutthroat, and nothing she did would ever convince her she would be. But according to Paula, there was no prestige in simply writing travel articles. To be taken seriously in this career, one had to stick her neck out. She had to take risks, to write articles that impacted the world. How could Madelyn argue with that?

After a moment of silent contemplation by Madelyn, Paula spoke. "Madelyn, remember what that cop did to your parents. Did he get justice? No. People need consequences. That's one of the problems with the world today. Everyone's babied, so they think they can get away with wronging other people. It's not right. People need to take responsibility for their actions. That cop who killed your parents needs to take responsibility. Zach Davis needs to own up to what he did and face the consequences. Do you understand?"

Paula's pep talk—if that's what it could be called— kicked Madelyn into gear. Her friend was right. This was no time to be a chicken. This was her time to shine. "Okay. I'm on it."

"Just think about what this can do for you. This would put you in the big league. Just like Wilcox Industries did for me."

Paula had broken the story about a board member with Wilcox Industries who was embezzling money from the power company and therefore had been embezzling from investors. After her article went viral, Paula had been nominated for awards for her fearless reporting. It was one of the reasons she'd made editor in chief of a popular magazine at only thirty-six years old. The fact that she'd seen something in Madelyn meant the world to her. Madelyn might not ever get another chance like this again. She had to seize the opportunity while she could.

Madelyn felt more determined now than ever.

"You sent the right person, Paula. I'm going to write the story of my life. My feelings won't get in the way of doing what's right and what's necessary."

"That's my girl. Now, go knock this exposé out of the park."

Madelyn hit End on her cell phone. She had to push through her doubts and do what needed to be done. But what a start to her stay here.

She didn't even like being center of attention. That's why she liked reporting so much—it allowed her to be in the background, yet to make a difference. Paula, on the other hand, should have gone into broadcast journalism. She loved to be in the spotlight.

Madelyn set her phone on the kitchen counter, staring at her temporary home. It was really a lovely, contemporary space. The kitchen had stainless steel appliances. The furniture all looked exotic, like it had been imported with its heavy wood frames and intricate designs. The walls had a Caribbean vibe with their mango, lime and pineapple colors.

She took a deep breath and gathered her courage. She had to be tough and strong if she was going to stay in this town and tackle her first big assignment.

With that thought, she walked across the hardwood floor toward the living room. She opened the door, revealing a huge, second-story porch. Stunning views of the bay waited there. Despite the cool breeze that swept inside— no doubt chillier because of the wind brushing over the water—Madelyn took a step out.

When she did, she sucked in a deep breath. It was beautiful here, and the duplex allowed a top-notch view of the water.

Her parents had always talked to her about God making the heavens and the earth. About nature declaring the majesty of God. About God being the ultimate creative and Creator.

Madelyn had stopped believing in God a long time ago, though, right about the time her parents had died. No loving God would ever allow a tragedy like that, and nothing anyone ever told her would change her mind. College had only confirmed her suspicions. Intellect and reason were the route to go if she wanted to find true satisfaction in life.

Her parents had been good people. Madelyn had been a good girl, for that matter, someone who'd always tried to follow the rules. What had she gotten as a reward? Nothing but pain and hardship. That's when she'd decided to throw herself completely into her career. If not God, what else was there to live for? She certainly didn't want to put her faith in romance or finding the right man. Paula had been through enough bad relationships to prove that point. Madelyn had dated a lot herself, but the process just seemed futile. She couldn't really see herself spending forever with any of the men she met.

With a bitter taste now in her mouth, Madelyn scanned the shoreline. Her gaze came to a stop as something reflected the moonlight. What *was* that glimmer?

She tensed as she looked more closely. She wasn't sure why the glare had caught her eye, but she had to trust her gut. Something out of the ordinary stirred her instincts.

She walked to the corner of the porch, leaning in to get a better look. That's when the gleam disappeared.

What?

She held her breath, watching for a clue. The glare had come from near the public pier that stretched into the water not far from the house.

She saw movement. Almost a shadow blowing in the wind. But that was no shadow. The movements were too purposeful.

It was a man crouching as he crept away from the pier.

And he'd been holding binoculars, she realized.

Someone was spying on her.

Her heart leaped into her throat at the realization, and fear shuddered through her.

She'd just arrived in town, but she knew one thing for sure: she was in trouble.

FOUR

Zach knocked on Madelyn's door after receiving her frantic phone call. She'd told Lynn—the dispatcher—that a man had been watching her from the beach and that he could be connected with the earlier incidents. Zach had still been at the police station when the call came in, so the trip to Madelyn's place had been quick.

She jerked the door open and stepped back. Her arms were wrapped across her chest, her eyes had that dazed, wide-eyed look and her breathing seemed too shallow. The woman was honestly scared, he realized. This wasn't a game or a cry for attention or any of the other possibilities that had wandered through his mind.

"Thanks for coming." Madelyn tugged her beige sweater closer around her neck. "I'm sorry. I'm not always a damsel in distress. I don't know what's going on here."

Zach didn't know what was happening either, but he would love some answers. "Again, the only thing we can assume is that it sounds like someone doesn't want you here in Waterman's Reach. And I have to ask once more, any idea why?"

She frowned. "Haven't we been through this? And shouldn't you be looking for the man who was watching me out there instead of interrogating me?"

He hooked his hand on his gun belt and nodded toward

the water beyond the house. "I already searched the beach on my way here. Whoever was there is long gone. He probably went to his car and drove off as soon as he realized he'd been spotted."

"Or he went to his white truck." Madelyn raised her eyebrows, waiting for him to follow her chain of thoughts.

"Or his white truck," he conceded before shifting his stance. "Look, Madelyn, I'm sorry. I know this can't be easy on you, but I assure you we're doing everything we can to find the person responsible. This isn't normal for Waterman's Reach."

She offered a stiff nod, still not appearing totally convinced. "I appreciate it."

"Can I come in a moment?"

"Of course."

As she moved aside, he stepped into the duplex and followed behind her up a set of stairs into the living area above. He needed to find out more information so he could write a report.

Madelyn paused between the combined kitchen and dining room. "Can I get you some coffee? I think there's some around here."

Zach started to refuse but changed his mind. "If you wouldn't mind, I would love some. It's been a long day."

"I wonder why." Her voice was tinged with sarcasm as she went into the kitchen and began fiddling with the coffeepot. A couple of minutes later, a fresh pot was perking.

She came over to the kitchen table, where he sat. The sleeves of her oversized sweater were pulled down over her hands, almost like she was using the clothing as a blanket. She lowered herself into the chair across from him.

He leaned toward her. "Madelyn, I need to ask you some questions so we can narrow down what's going on here. Obviously someone has you in his crosshairs—figuratively, of course."

She frowned. "Of course."

"I can't believe at this point that this is random—that someone simply saw you driving down Lankford Highway, decided to follow you and this chain of events is a result."

"I agree that sounds like a stretch. But I really don't have any good ideas for you."

"Usually in cases like this, we look at the people closest to you. I know you said there's no boyfriend or ex-boyfriend. But maybe you have an admirer or even an ex-boyfriend who's in your distant past, whom you haven't heard from in years."

She stood as the coffee finished perking, grabbed a mug and poured a cup for him. "Cream or sugar?"

"Just black. Thanks."

She brought him the drink and grabbed a cup for herself before sitting down again. Tight lines stretched across her face, and her movements looked stiff, almost stoic.

She sighed before saying, "I really have no idea. I haven't had any serious boyfriends. I have no secret admirers. I have no blatant admirers for that matter. I mostly just have my career."

Zach found that hard to believe. He'd guess there were plenty of guys who wouldn't mind dating someone like Madelyn Sawyer. She was pretty, her eyes were kind and when she smiled it could take someone's breath away. The woman was probably so focused on her career that she didn't notice. She seemed like the driven type.

"Okay, how about family? Any arguments or fights or bad blood?"

She shook her head, her hands trembling against her coffee mug. "No, I have no family."

"None at all?" Certainly they were just estranged. She was too young to be all alone.

"None. I was an only child, and my parents died in a

car crash." It sounded like it took all of her energy just to say that.

Zach had the impulse to reach forward and grab Madelyn's hand. Of course he didn't. It wouldn't be professional. Instead, he said, "I'm sorry."

She nodded, but the action was tight. Grief shone in waves through her eyes. "Thank you."

He snapped back to the investigation, trying to push away any concern and to deny his strange urge to offer her comfort. "How about coworkers? Any of them have a grudge against you?"

She stared out the window a moment. "I write travel articles. It's not like I'm a critic who tears apart movies or restaurants. I don't write about crime. I help towns get business. The office staff is small. It's just me, my editor and a couple of other full-timers. Everyone else is freelance. We all get along."

He frowned. "So there's really no one? This doesn't give us much to go on."

Madelyn pulled her sleeves down farther over her hands and rubbed them together. She appeared so alone, so lost. "I'm sorry. I wish I had more. I haven't seen anything. I haven't talked to anyone or had any confrontations with strangers. I'm pretty sure I haven't even looked at anyone the wrong way."

"That sounds pretty thorough."

She frowned. "So what should I do? Should I listen to the man's threat and go home?"

"I can't make that decision for you." Part of Zach thought that sounded like the best idea of all. But there was no guarantee someone wouldn't follow her wherever she went. Plus, Zach never liked to give in to pressure caused by bullies.

He knew all about that.

He'd held his ground and ended up losing his job because of it.

Madelyn's eyelids drooped, and she still hadn't touched her coffee. She was exhausted, he realized. He stood, feeling like he'd done all he could do here.

"I should let you get some rest. Call me if you need me."

"Will do. Thank you again." She started to stand.

Zach held up a hand to stop her. "I can walk myself out. Really."

He lumbered down the steps. At the bottom landing, he saw a piece of paper that had fallen against the wall. He picked it up and started to call for Madelyn when the words there caught his eye.

"Zach B. Davis

30 years old

Originally from Richmond, Virginia."

Was this Madelyn's? Why would the regional reporter have personal information written out about him? Wasn't she here to do a travel piece on the town?

His back muscles suddenly went rigid. She may come off as being kind and sweet, but that didn't mean she was.

He needed to keep an eye on Madelyn Sawyer, that was for sure. One wrong move, and she could ruin everything.

Madelyn had awakened the next morning with a new determination to investigate Zach Davis. When he'd shown up at her duplex last night, she'd found herself softening, opening up. She had to remember her mission—she needed to put professional distance between her and the subject of her article.

She glanced across the beach now. The sun set in the distance, streaking royal colors across the sky. She was a guest of honor at an oyster roast. The event was amazing. Mayor Alan was hosting it at his place, which was located on a long, private stretch of beach. A band played on a makeshift stage closer to the house, tables full of seafood had been laid out and people were readily engaging in the feast there. The smell of seafood, unappealing when she'd first arrived in town, now seemed alluring.

She'd spent the day with Eva Rogers, the town's publicity manager, and had taken a tour of the retail area. They'd gone in various shops that featured items from local artists. They'd had coffee at The Java House. Then lunch at a seafood restaurant called Jim Buoy's.

Later, a horse and carriage had eased them down the town's streets and offered amazing views of some of the character-rich homes. A historian had joined them and had given Madelyn an account of the town from all the way back in the day when the area had been a bustling port and a playground for wealthy hunters and fishermen.

Despite herself, Madelyn was fascinated by everything she learned. She hadn't thought she'd enjoy hearing about or seeing the town like she did. But the community was quaint and friendly and had something Madelyn had been seeking for her entire adult life: belonging. Her car had even been personally delivered back to her today with a note that the repair was "on the house."

If she would allow herself to forget about the threats she'd encountered since leaving Maryland for the sleepy town, she might actually enjoy this place. Those things remained in the back of her mind, though. As did the real reason for her being here.

She glanced across the crowd again and spotted the one person she'd come to town to research. Zach Davis.

He was here at the oyster roast, talking with a group of people near the large grill. He'd dressed casually in jeans and a well-fitting T-shirt. He didn't seem like the life-of-the-party type, but instead he stood back, engaging in the conversations around him in an easy-going manner.

His back was never toward the crowd, and she'd caught him scanning his environment several times.

He seemed calm and steady, not the least bit impulsive or flighty, Madelyn mused. Maybe he hadn't always been like this. Maybe he'd sobered after the fiasco in Baltimore. She couldn't draw her conclusions too quickly, though. Even if she'd come into town with a different image of the man than the one he presented, that didn't mean he was innocent.

As he glanced up, she quickly looked away.

"He's quite handsome, isn't he?" Eva suddenly appeared at her side. She carried a plate of oysters in one hand and a tall, dewy glass of a cheerful-looking drink in the other.

Eva was probably in her midfifties and had short brown hair that seemed to poof around her face. The woman had a quick smile and a bubbly personality that had made Madelyn feel right at home.

Madelyn shrugged, desperate not to give herself away, and took a sip of her lemon water. "I suppose."

"We're all so excited to have him here. He's done an outstanding job so far."

"Where'd he come from?"

Eva tapped her lips. "Hmm…you know, I can't remember. But it was some other little town. Smuggler's Cove, I believe. It's a little island out in the bay."

"I can't imagine his job keeps him busy here."

"Oh, I'm sure it's boring, but that's the way we like it. Boring equals safe so we'll take it."

Suddenly, Madelyn straightened as she peered in the distance beyond Eva. A white pickup truck disappeared down the road and out of sight. She sucked in a deep breath at the sight, that fear that was becoming all too familiar coursing through her until her arms shook.

"Is everything okay?" Eva examined Madelyn with motherly concern.

Madelyn rubbed her neck and nodded. "Yes, of course."

Madelyn hadn't mentioned anything to Eva about last night—either about the snatched oysters or the binoculars she'd seen someone using outside her apartment. It was better if she kept any attention off herself.

And Zach obviously ran a tight ship. In most small towns, it would be easy for word to spread and for everyone to know other people's business. Zach seemed to have high standards. Had he encouraged those working under him to keep the incidents confidential?

"If it's not our favorite reporter," someone said.

Madelyn recognized the man as Mayor Alan. They'd been introduced briefly when she arrived at the oyster roast. The man had a thick blond mustache and matching hair that was graying on the edges. He had a solid build, a tanned complexion and a ready smile. His clothes screamed expensive and, based on everything she'd observed about him, he was wealthy. Maybe one of the wealthiest, most powerful people in town.

"Are you having a good time?" he asked.

"Yes, it seems like a great town you've got here." She scanned her surroundings again, waiting to see a figure lurking.

She was being paranoid. Certainly there were other white trucks here in town. She had to get a grip.

The sun was setting over the bay, and the sky was lit in deep reds and purples. In other circumstances, this would have been an enjoyable day. A perfect day for that matter.

But Madelyn couldn't relax. Not when so much was on the line.

She made chitchat with Eva and Mayor Alan, talking about the town and all of its charms and quirks. She tried to properly sell the idea that she was writing a travel article.

Just then, her phone buzzed. She pulled it out and looked down at the screen.

It's Chief Davis. I have an update for you, but I'd like to tell you in person. Can you meet me by the shed on the edge of the property?

The chief was texting her? She had given him her contact information yesterday in case he had any more questions. But this seemed almost unprofessional.

She glanced around, looking for the chief, but she didn't see him anywhere. Interesting.

"Could you excuse me a minute?" she asked Eva and Mayor Alan.

"Well of course!" the mayor said. "You're the guest of honor here. I know you have a lot of people you want to speak with while you're in town. Go right ahead."

With a touch of trepidation, she started toward the shed. She supposed there weren't many landmarks they could meet at besides on the beach. But unease continued to grow in her stomach with each step.

Did Zach Davis know why she was really here? Would he confront her? If he was as dangerous as Paula seemed to think, would he do more than confront her? Did he have the potential to…harm her?

She rubbed her hands on her linen pants as she reached the door. The sun sank below the horizon and sent another shiver down her spine.

In other circumstances, this would be romantic. Instead, she was alone. Was she always destined to be single? The question seemed both morbid and inconsequential. Paula always told her it was better to be alone. Having no plus-one meant freedom.

But Madelyn had seen what a good relationship her mother and father had, and she wanted that for her own life. She didn't want to see the world by herself. She wanted a partner by her side to share her struggles and to celebrate her victories.

She let out a sigh and continued trudging through the sand. She was probably wishing for too much, and that made her seem weak. She needed to be strong right now, especially if she was meeting the chief. Zach Davis was the type who could easily see through facades. His gaze made it clear that he was always analyzing things around them. That would include Madelyn. The thought made her nervous. What if he could see through her? What would she do then?

She reached the shed, but no one was there. She glanced around. The crowds from the oyster roast were on the other side of the beach, far away from this building, which was set back on the grassy banks, away from the sand.

Where was Chief Davis? She searched the crowds in the distance again but didn't spot him.

Impatient, she peered around the back side of the building. When she did, a masked man lunged at her from the shadows.

In an instant, her life flashed before her eyes.

FIVE

Madelyn struggled against the man in black—her captor. She thrashed, trying to get out of his grip. She tried to scream, but a gloved hand went over her mouth.

"I warned you," the man grumbled.

Just hearing his gravelly voice ratcheted her fear to the next level. She thrashed even harder. She used her elbows to catch the man's ribs. She kicked at his shins.

It was no use. He was stronger than she was and easily overpowered her. All of Madelyn's efforts seemed futile.

She wasn't ready to give up, though. She craned her neck, straining to catch a glance at her captor. His face was covered with a black mask, making him unrecognizable.

Had this been Zach all along? Had he secretly followed Madelyn into town and pretended someone else shot at him in the woods yesterday? Had he disguised his voice so she wouldn't recognize him? He was the only person in town who'd known she was at her duplex alone last night. He'd had enough time to change before coming back and trying to run her out of town as she stood there on the stoop. He could have even been down by the pier with binoculars. The dispatcher had answered when she called, so Zach would have enough time to change again. Right now he could be concealing his face and trying to scare her out of town.

The man raised her off her feet and edged her toward the shed.

No!

She glanced down, trying to get any kind of clue as to who he might be. All she could see were his shoes. Black, glossy, sandy. She tried to memorize what she could.

In one motion, he tossed her into the shed. Her backside ached on impact, and the sudden motion caused a shovel to fall, landing hard on her hand.

"Go home," the man growled as he leered into the darkness. She could only see the whites of his eyes, and that was enough to turn her stomach with fear.

Then he was gone. Blackness surrounded her. Something scraped outside the door.

The lock, she realized. The man had locked her in here.

Coming to her senses, she scrambled to her feet. Already, imaginary spiders were crawling across her skin. Her body let out an involuntary tremble as fear rose in her.

Alone…the word echoed in her head. The thought caused adrenaline to surge in her.

She pounded at the door. "Let me out of here!"

She stopped after several minutes and listened.

Between the music playing on the beach and everyone milling around eating oysters and other seafood, what were the chances that someone would hear her? Or even come looking for her? Eva might just assume she'd gone back to her apartment. It was a logical assumption since it was getting late.

She'd call for help, except she must have dropped her purse when the man grabbed her. Her phone had been tucked inside.

She banged on the door again, trying hard to get someone's attention. "Please, help me!"

She waited, but there was nothing.

She pressed her forehead against the door a moment,

trying to collect herself before she fell completely apart. She hated the dark. She hated confined spaces. She hated being alone.

Don't think like that. Get focused. Come up with solutions.

Had Zach Davis locked her in here? Had he lured her to the shed and tried to scare her? Maybe he knew her real reason for being in town and needed to stop her. He was the most logical choice because he had the most to lose.

But how would he have found out Madelyn's true intentions? Had he felt intimidated because he knew she was from Baltimore?

That realization ignited something in her. If Zach thought he would bully her into leaving, he was wrong. She was going to fight until the end.

She hit the door again, harder this time. "Please, help me!"

With no one responding still, she crossed her arms protectively over her chest. She glanced around, but it was too dark to see anything inside the small space. It smelled like gasoline and oil and lawn equipment. And though it was balmy outside, the inside of this shed was stuffy and humid after collecting heat all day.

How long would she be in here? What if no one found her? This space wasn't large enough for the grill she'd seen outside. For all she knew, no one ever came out here except for the maintenance man on occasion.

That thought made her throat tighten.

No, she couldn't think worst-case scenarios. She had to stay positive. Worrying would only pull her under.

Therefore do not worry about tomorrow, for tomorrow will worry about itself. Each day has enough trouble of its own.

She hadn't thought of that verse from Matthew in a long time. Not since she'd been to church with her parents when she was a teenager. That had been ten years ago, yet at once the memories seemed so strong.

The ache in her chest deepened.

Would her parents be proud of her now? She couldn't imagine them approving of her going undercover for a story. Though she considered her alias a cover and this whole scenario an effort for the greater good, her parents would consider it a lie.

Paula always said her parents sounded too stuffy and saw things too much in black-and-white. Madelyn couldn't quite bring herself to believe that, though.

As the music continued outside the shed, Madelyn sank to the wooden floor.

Maybe Zach Davis was desperate to maintain his good reputation in the community. The only way to keep up this ruse was to get rid of Madelyn. She had no idea how he would have found what she was really up to. But he was probably resourceful.

Okay, Madelyn. Think.

She was in a shed. Certainly there were tools in here, some type of resource she could use to escape.

Blindly, she began feeling the space around her. Finally, she felt what she thought was a hammer. Could she bang her way out of here?

She didn't have many options, so she decided to give it a shot. She pounded the tool against the wood, trying to make as much noise as possible.

"Please help me!"

Just then she heard a rustling on the other side. Had the man come back? Was he determined to keep her quiet once and for all?

She raised the hammer, determined not to be a victim.

The door opened.

The man standing on the other side caused her blood to go cold.

* * *

Zach blinked with surprise when he saw Madelyn Sawyer inside the shed with a hammer raised above her head. He thought he'd heard a noise coming from the building as he walked back to his truck. But he'd never expected this.

Madelyn looked frightened and rightfully so. Why was she in the shed with an unclasped padlock holding the door shut?

Before he could ask, she scrambled out, moving so frantically that she tumbled into his arms. As quickly as his hands went to her waist, she pulled back, obviously flustered. She raised the hammer again.

Her hands were shaking and her knuckles bleeding. Her normally well-placed hair looked disheveled. But that was nothing compared to the panic in her gaze.

The brief moment of relief in her eyes quickly turned to anger. Anger over what?

His concern morphed into curiosity.

"You can put the hammer down," he urged, realizing how ugly this could turn.

The outrage remained in her gaze. "How do I know I can trust you?"

"I'm not going to hurt you, Madelyn. Please, put the hammer down. Assaulting the police chief isn't the way you want to start your stay here."

At that moment, she looked down at his feet. He followed her gaze and glanced at his tan boat shoes. Something about his footwear must have reassured her because she dropped the hammer on the ground and squeezed the skin between her eyes.

"What are you doing in the shed?" He felt like he should reach out to her, to reassure her, to offer some kind of comfort in the midst of her frightened state. But he also sensed that she would reject any touch he offered. For that reason, Zach stayed back, trying to give her space and time to compose herself as the sounds of the party continued to murmur in the background.

"I just thought I would check it out for my article." She straightened her clothes—now stained—and raised her chin, some of her pride returning. She'd pushed aside her broken state, and determination now stained her gaze.

She started past him, but Zach grabbed her arm. Had a crime happened here? He couldn't just pretend like he hadn't seen any of this. He had a duty to the law. "No, really. I need to know what's going on."

She turned toward him, heat in her gaze.

It wasn't the normal reaction he received after he'd helped someone. But nothing about Madelyn seemed normal. Not her uneasiness, her beauty, her interactions with him.

"A man locked me in there," she said, her voice low and hard. "I don't suppose you know anything about it?"

Surprise flashed through him. Was she accusing him? "Why would I know anything about it?"

She grabbed her purse, which was lying outside the shed like she'd dropped it, and reached inside. A moment later, she shoved her phone in his face. "Does this text message look familiar?"

His eyes widened as he read the words there. "That's not my number, and I never sent that text to you."

"Sure it's not."

As she started to storm away again, he gently touched her arm. Compassion echoed through him as he realized she was frightened and shaken. The implications of what had happened washed over him. "No, really. It's not my number, Madelyn. Look at my phone if you want."

She stared at him a moment, as if trying to figure out if he was telling the truth. "How do I know you don't have two phones?"

He shrugged. "I suppose you don't."

"Tell me why someone would send me a text and put your name in it?"

"That's a good question. For some reason, someone wants to ensure that you don't trust me."

She stepped closer, challenge in her gaze. "Is that because you're trying to hide something?"

His cheeks warmed with irritation. She was overstepping her boundaries—big time. "You need to tread carefully, Ms. Sawyer."

"Is that a threat?" Her hands went to her hips.

That text message had done its job, it appeared, because the woman obviously didn't have any faith in him.

"By no means is it a threat. I just think you're not doing yourself any favors storming into town and making accusations."

Flames lit in her eyes just as fireworks began exploding over the water. "What am I supposed to think?"

He crossed his arms, growing agitated. "I suppose you should consider that someone must really not want you here."

"Exactly!"

"But why?" Why would someone feel this threatened by her? That's what didn't make sense. He'd asked himself that question many times since her arrival in town. There were obviously things about Madelyn Sawyer that he didn't know yet. He had to keep prodding until he found some answers. "What aren't you telling me?"

"Isn't it your job to figure out why this is happening?"

They stared at each other another moment. Tension crackled between them. He didn't usually have such explosive encounters with pretty newcomers in town. In fact, most people thought he was levelheaded. But there was something about Madelyn that brought out a different side of him.

"Oh, there you are!"

Zach's shoulders tightened even more. He knew who the voice belonged to. Eva. She had the worst timing possible. Or maybe it was the best. Who knew where the conversation would have gone otherwise.

"Hi, Eva," Madelyn muttered.

"Good evening," Zach said, following suit.

Eva looked between the two of them a moment, as if sensing she'd just interrupted something.

"Well…" she said slowly with a clap of her hands. "I'm glad I caught you together. I have good news. The two of you are going to do a ride along together tomorrow."

Zach glanced over his shoulder toward Madelyn, half expecting her to be scowling. Instead, she nodded stiffly, confirming that she was okay with this.

"I have a busy day," Zach said, not missing a beat.

Eva laughed and flopped her hand in the air, seeming not to hear him. "Oh, you. I think this will be a great angle for the story. Mayor Alan said you wouldn't mind, Chief. You said you were willing to do what you needed to help promote tourism in the town."

She had him there. Zach had said that, but he'd had no idea when he made that promise that Madelyn Sawyer would sweep into town with all of her judgment and accusations.

He glanced at the woman again. Maybe this would be a good chance for him to dig into her background. She was definitely hiding something. He was more certain now than ever. "You're right. I did promise the mayor that. I'll pick you up at eight?"

Something flashed in Madelyn's eyes. Eagerness? Anticipation? Finally, she nodded. "That sounds good, Chief."

But as unsettled as he felt, he couldn't forget what had happened to her tonight. Someone had locked her in a shed away from the crowds. Why would someone do that? Who could be so desperate to keep this woman out of Waterman's Reach?

He didn't know. But he needed to find out.

SIX

Madelyn didn't want to do this. She had no desire to spend more time with Zach Davis. But she was sent here to do a job, and that meant she couldn't shy away from this opportunity. That's why she'd suggested a ride along with the chief.

It would be the perfect chance to dig a little deeper into Zach's past. She should be thankful that the opportunity had presented itself while she was talking to the mayor at the oyster roast last night.

She shivered as she waited on the stoop outside her temporary home for Zach to arrive. She'd hardly gotten any sleep last night. Every time she thought about everything that had happened since she'd arrived, her stomach sank. Someone desperately wanted to scare her and get her out of town.

But there was so much that didn't make sense about that. All of her conclusions came back to one man—Zach Davis. He had the most to lose, so he was the most likely culprit. But he hadn't been wearing shiny black shoes last night. If she could find the person who had been, maybe she could find some answers concerning the various mysteries that had arisen since she'd arrived here.

Finally, the chief's cruiser pulled up. Before Zach

could even get out, she opened the passenger side door and climbed inside without fanfare.

"Good morning," Zach said. He looked like he felt as uncomfortable as she did. His neck muscles flexed beneath his collared shirt. His shoulders were set and uptight.

He was doing this out of obligation to the mayor, she realized.

Madelyn clicked her seat belt in place. "I know you're busy, so just pretend I'm not here. I'm only along for the ride, to get your perspective on the town."

"Good morning to you, too. I brought you some coffee, sugar and cream on the side." He nodded to the paper cup in the holder near her chair.

Madelyn's muscles relaxed a moment. How could someone so thoughtful be a suspect in her mind? No. She couldn't let his kindness—or illusion of kindness—sway her.

"You don't like coffee?" he asked.

She snapped back to reality, realizing she hadn't responded. "No, I do. Thank you. And good morning."

Silence stretched a moment as he pulled away from the house. Madelyn didn't know what to say, and small talk wasn't coming easily at the moment. Instead, she took a sip of her drink. It was warm and just what she needed to help her wake up.

"I just wanted to let you know that I did ask around last night after the shed incident," the chief said. "No one saw anything. The phone number that the text message was sent from, under my name, was one of those disposable phones that anyone can get. They're untraceable."

Madelyn frowned. Of course no one had seen anything. And every criminal seemed to know about burner phones that they could buy at drugstores and dispose of before the police could trace them thanks to TV shows and crime novels.

Whoever had shoved her in the shed knew exactly what he was doing. He was experienced...just like the chief.

She cleared her throat. *Get in his good graces*, she reminded herself. *That's the best way to find answers.*

"I appreciate you following up," she finally said.

Silence stretched between them again.

"Look, I know that text was signed with my name, but like I said last night, I didn't send it," Zach finally said.

"That's good to know."

Suddenly, her throat tightened. Ahead, a white truck pulled off a road and onto a side street. This couldn't be a coincidence. She'd seen that truck one too many times. Too many bad things had happened in connection with it.

As she remembered what it had been like in that dark shed last night, she trembled, fear threatening to overtake her. This wasn't over yet, was it? As long as she stayed here, she would be in danger.

Was this article worth it?

Zach must have spotted the truck also because he accelerated. "That's the guy who followed you, isn't it?"

"I can't be positive, but so it appears."

"Let's find out once and for all who's in that driver's seat." He sped up, cruising down the road toward the other vehicle.

Madelyn wasn't sure if she felt relieved or even more paranoid. She wanted answers. What she didn't want was to look like a fool in front of the chief. If this was the wrong truck or if all of this was a coincidence, then he'd never take her seriously. She'd look like she was just trying to stir up trouble.

As they rounded a bend in the road, the truck had disappeared. An empty street stared back at them. It was like the vehicle had vanished into thin air.

"Where did it go?" Madelyn whispered.

"I suppose the driver could have gone down any of these

roads." He pointed to three different streets that branched from the main one. Each one was surrounded by trees, and it was impossible to see very far down them.

She bit back a frown. Until she knew who was behind the attacks on her, she wouldn't feel safe.

Just then, the chief's radio crackled. Zach spoke into a mouthpiece on his shoulder, but Madelyn couldn't make out everything being said. The next instant, he did a U-turn.

"Someone just reported that the back door to my house is open," he said. "I'm going to swing by my place and make sure everything is okay."

"Sure thing."

They cruised down the country road and, a few minutes later, pulled up to a tiny bungalow on the edge of the water. "Excuse me one minute."

Zach slipped inside his house.

Madelyn paced outside, trying to keep her thoughts focused. She observed his house for a moment. It was more of a cinder block cottage, really. Pale yellow siding and a neat white porch greeted visitors. There was an American flag waving in the breeze in the front yard.

It didn't look like the home of someone with nefarious intentions.

She let out a sigh, frustrated with herself. Why was she going back and forth so much about the chief? One minute she couldn't stand him and the next she was sure he was innocent. She needed to stick with her convictions.

When Zach didn't come out after several minutes, her interest spiked. Out of curiosity, she walked around to the back door to see what was going on.

The door was closed, and she didn't see any damage outside. Perhaps the wind had just blown the door open. That didn't explain why Zach was still inside.

Before Madelyn could second-guess herself, she stepped onto the back deck and peered in through the glass portion of the back door to make sure he was okay. What she saw there made her freeze.

Chief Davis stood at the kitchen counter surrounded by blood.

Zach stared at the blood spread across his kitchen counter. There was a lot of it. It pooled around the sink and dripped onto the floor. Parts were smeared, other parts spattered. All of it painted a grisly picture of…murder.

What in the world had happened? How had this gotten here, in his house? Zach had only been gone a few hours.

His stomach clenched. Someone had been here. They'd left this for him to see. They'd left it for a reason, to make a statement.

This was just one of many messages someone had been trying to send Zach. Did they want to run him out of town? To damage his reputation? Both?

Even more concerning to him than that was the reality of this blood. Had it come from a human? If so, where was this person right now?

Could he or she be somewhere in his home?

Behind him, someone drew in a quick breath. Zach swung around and spotted Madelyn standing there, a horrified expression on her face as she stared at the scene in front of her.

The conclusions she must be drawing were similar to his. Except for one thing: Zach knew he had nothing to do with this. Madelyn did not.

"This isn't what it looks like." He pulled his eyes away from Madelyn and absorbed the scene again. Cheerful sunlight streamed through the window, betraying the truth about the atrocity that had happened here. One way or another, a crime had been committed here. He just wasn't sure about the extent of it yet.

Madelyn took a step back. "What have you done?"

He raised his hand, trying to calm her. When he saw the blood on his own fingers, he realized just how guilty he looked. This was worse than he'd imagined.

"Madelyn, I didn't do anything," he told her. "It looked like this when I walked in here."

Her eyes were wide and full of fear and doubt. "Why should I believe you?"

"Why wouldn't you believe me? You think if I did this that I would bring you back here to see it? What purpose would that serve?" He hoped his attempt to reason with her would work.

"I'm not sure. It sounds like something a psycho might get his kicks out of."

She had a point.

"I didn't do this," he repeated. "I value life."

Madelyn's gaze softened. Maybe his words had gotten through to her. She licked her lips, as if still reserving her judgment.

"Where'd the blood come from?" Her voice was so soft he had to strain to hear her. She pulled her hand up over her mouth and stared at the crimson behind him. Part of it dripped on the floor, forming a pool on the tile. Another area had been smeared across part of his back door.

"I'm not sure where it came from," he told her. "I need you to wait here while I check out the rest of the house and make sure there's nothing else I need to know about. Don't touch anything. Do you understand? This is now a crime scene."

She crossed her arms but nodded. Taking a step back, her gaze seemed riveted on the horror around her. It was enough to shake anyone up.

Moving carefully through the house, Zach checked every room. Each appeared untouched. The only sign that someone had been in here was that blood on his kitchen counter, sink and back door.

But that didn't make sense. If someone was injured in his house, the blood pattern would have been different. It would tell a story of struggle and fighting.

Instead, this blood almost looked like it had been placed there.

Had someone known that Madelyn was with him? Had that person planted this blood, left the door open and then called dispatch in order to ensure that Madelyn saw it?

The only reason he could think that someone would do this was to raise suspicions about him. Was that why they sent that text with his name attached also? To make him look bad?

His fears surged closer to the surface. Initially, he'd thought that maybe one of the locals wanted to run him out of town. They wanted one of their own to be the chief instead of an outsider. That would explain his slashed tires, the broken pottery and the dead fish.

But what if one of the people from Baltimore who hated him, who thought he was guilty of taking someone's life, knew he was here and wanted to make him pay for the crime he had supposedly committed? What if they believed in *an eye for an eye*? Since Zach had taken a person's life in the drug bust, what if someone wanted to take his? Was this just a warning of what was to come?

Or a third theory came to mind. What if someone here knew his true reasons for coming into town? What if this person knew he was investigating Waterman's Reach as the potential drop spot for an international drug ring? Raking his name through the mud would be a surefire way of getting him out of town and ceasing his investigation.

When Zach came back into the kitchen, Madelyn was standing over the counter, peering at the blood. He still needed to take pictures, to document everything before it was compromised.

"Don't touch anything," he instructed her again.

"I wasn't going to," she said, an edge to her voice. She stepped back, her hands in the air. "Did you find something?"

Zach shook his head, trying to piece together what might have happened, as he walked toward the front door. "No, nothing. I don't know what kind of stunt someone is trying to pull here, but I'm not amused. I need you to wait in the car."

"What are you doing?"

"I've got to take photos, as well as collect some samples, dust for fingerprints, search for a sign of how someone got inside. If something happened in my home, I need to find out what."

The more he thought about it, the more he wondered if the blood was even human.

One thing he knew for sure: something was fishy. And there was no way he was going to let his investigation be compromised. No way.

SEVEN

Zach pulled to a stop in front of Madelyn's apartment and put his cruiser in Park. He'd collected all of his evidence, dropped it by the office and now he needed to head back there and process everything.

"Sorry today was a bit unexpected," he started.

Of all the days that Madelyn was tagging along with him, it had to be today. When news of this got back to the mayor, he wouldn't be happy.

But Zach had bigger issues at hand right now.

"I hope you get everything figured out," she said before climbing out and disappearing inside her apartment.

Madelyn still looked freaked out, like a seed of doubt had been planted in her mind concerning his innocence. Someone was working hard to make sure that was the case.

Someone had also attempted to make sure Baltimore looked like his blunder. Whether it was his fault or not, the guilt of what had happened there still haunted him every day. The gang members had been waiting for officers to arrive. When they had shown up, it was open season. Two officers had been shot and killed.

He'd had no choice but to fire back on the gang, hitting one of the members and killing him.

Though he'd been legally acquitted of all wrongdoing, the trial by the public had been hard to recover from. He'd stepped down from his job, knowing it was best for the department and overall morale within local enforcement, as each of their moves had been scrutinized.

It would be best if you got out of town.

He remembered Julia's words. His ex-fiancée had turned on him and decided that looking out for her own interests would be best for both of them. Apparently, she was having trouble in her social circles since her name was connected with his.

Eventually, she'd decided to use the whole situation to her advantage. She'd grabbed up her fifteen minutes of fame, going on both local news stations and eventually working her way up to a few national reports, as well. Why hadn't he been able to see through her sooner? He'd had no idea that she'd drop her loyalty toward him so easily. He'd been willing to spend the rest of his life with her.

Maybe it was a good thing that God had allowed the situation to show Julia's true colors before they tied the knot.

But her sting of betrayal still hurt.

He sighed and thought about everything that had transpired over the past couple of days. What a bad time for the plucky reporter to be in town and to be doing a ride along. He still didn't quite trust the woman. He felt certain she was hiding something. But what?

And what was the big deal about that white truck they'd seen earlier?

There were many things that didn't make sense. He needed to remain on guard around her. He'd staked everything on being here. Months of research. Sleepless nights. The heroin that had been central in the drug ring up in Baltimore was somehow connected with Waterman's Reach. Someone here was involved in smuggling it in from overseas and then transporting it up the coast.

He was still trying to pinpoint who and where. Most of

his free time was spent watching the coast, wandering the docks and talking to local fisherman who might have a clue.

Of course, no one here would betray another local. Their loyalty went deep, and they would refuse to snitch, so he could only hope that someone would slip up and spill something they intended to keep quiet.

Just then, in the distance, Zach saw that white pickup truck again—the one that Madelyn had pointed out earlier. Interesting. Was it really following Madelyn? Was the driver somehow connected with the incident in the woods, the attack on her first night here and locking her in the shed yesterday?

It was his best lead.

Zach straightened and watched the vehicle. The driver moved slowly, almost as if he were looking for someone. He went down Main Street, headed toward Madelyn's apartment. Just as Madelyn had said, the windows were tinted and there was a dent in the front bumper. Even the license plate appeared to be covered with mud, so much that he couldn't make out what state the plates were from. Virginia or Maryland?

Zach started the car, ready to follow the truck. He'd just put the car in Drive when Madelyn came running outside.

"Someone's been in my apartment," she said, her voice breathless.

Yes, something was definitely going on since she'd arrived.

As if to confirm his realization, a gunshot rang out.

"Get down!" he shouted.

Zach leaped from the car. He ran toward Madelyn, desperate to protect her. She turned around, almost as if in slow motion. The expression on her face went from confusion to horror as she realized what was happening.

He only hoped he reached her before it was too late.

* * *

Madelyn's heart slammed into her ribcage as gunfire pierced the air. The next thing she knew, Zach flew from the car and pushed her to the ground. She was all too aware of him hovering over her, his broad frame covering her.

"Stay down," he mumbled.

Her muscles tightened at his nearness, at his willingness to protect her. They hardly knew each other.

He was just doing his job, she reminded herself. It wasn't like he cared about her. Criminal, she reminded herself. He was a criminal.

Another gunshot cracked through the air, sending her heart skittering into overtime. This wasn't good. No, this was not good at all.

"It's going to be okay," Zach muttered into her ear.

Her blood warmed at his assurances.

"I need to get you behind my police cruiser. Okay?"

Move? He wanted her to move? She preferred to stay safe right where she was, at least until the danger had passed. But she'd have to trust Zach's judgment here. She nodded, but her trembling hands certainly gave away her fear.

"On the count of three," Zach said. "One, two, three!"

With Zach's help, Madelyn pulled herself from the ground. It was only five steps to reach the cruiser, but those steps felt like a mile. She pressed herself against the side of the car as Zach drew his gun and peered over the hood, searching for the shooter.

Just as he did, another bullet pierced the air.

Someone was shooting at them in broad daylight. That had to signal some type of desperation. The risk they were taking, their chances of being spotted and identified, increased exponentially without the cover of darkness.

All of this was too much—too much to comprehend, to piece together, to make sense of.

A car squealed off in the distance and finally Zach turned to her, assessing her with his gaze. "Are you okay?"

His eyes were full of concern, so much so that her skin pricked with awareness. She looked away from him before he could see her flush, concentrating instead on wiping the dirt from her pants. "I think I'm fine. You?"

He nodded, pulling his gaze from her and glancing around. "I'm going to have to check out your apartment in a minute. For now, I need you to get in the car."

She didn't argue. She climbed in. But her hands were shaking as she pulled on her seat belt.

Everything that had happened had shaken her, and for good reason. Was someone trying to kill her? Or just scare her out of town? At first, she wanted to think it was the chief. But obviously he wasn't responsible this time.

Her first thought was the white truck. Is that where the bullets had come from?

Zach pulled onto the street and turned on his lights. He flew through town, headed in the direction of his house.

"Where are we going?" She gripped the armrest.

"We're following the shooter."

Her eyes widened. "You saw him?"

"I saw a white truck. I need to find out where it went."

She gripped the seat and held on as his speed increased. As he drove, he radioed Lynn and told her to send Tyler to the shooting scene.

That white truck was connected to this, Madelyn realized. Thank goodness the chief had been there. Otherwise, she might be dead.

She glanced at him now. His eyes were focused on the road. His jaw muscles looked tight. His grip on the steering wheel showed white knuckles. Yet he seemed in control and measured.

Not like the kind of person who lost his head and shot

someone or incited violence or was secretly involved in a drug ring.

He turned onto a side street, the one the truck had disappeared on earlier. The road before them was empty. Zach tried the first street they came to. He sped down the wooded road, looking for the truck.

He searched the next three streets, but the truck was nowhere to be seen.

Finally, Zach pulled up to his house, put the cruiser in Park and sat silently.

Fear shot through her. She remembered the blood on his counter. Remembered the possibility that he was a killer. And all she wanted to do was run.

"What kind of game are you playing, Madelyn?" Zach's voice sounded deep and accusatory.

She'd known this was a good possibility. The man was obviously perceptive. How was she going to get out of this? Would she be able to convince him that she was writing a travel article? Her doubts taunted her.

Madelyn snapped her head toward Zach. "Excuse me?"

His gaze narrowed. "What aren't you telling me?"

"Nothing. What are you talking about?" Her voice trembled and betrayed her.

"Any idea why someone would be shooting at you? In broad daylight at that."

Her throat suddenly felt dry. "Are you sure they weren't shooting at you?"

"That bullet was aimed at you. Thankfully, this person wasn't a good shot, otherwise you'd be, at best, in the hospital right now."

She didn't ask where she'd be at worst. She already knew: she'd be dead.

"Is there anything you want to tell me?" he prodded.

Madelyn briefly considered pouring everything out to

him. The man had saved her life. And he seemed so trustworthy that she wanted to confide in him. It would be so nice to have someone to talk to about her fears.

But she had to focus on the bigger picture right now. She came here to do a job. Her heart was starting to mess all of that up.

"I have no idea why someone would want me dead. I'm just a reporter. I mostly do travel pieces, nothing too controversial. Your guess is as good as mine." She hoped her words sounded convincing. She rubbed her cheek as she formulated what to say next. "To be honest, I'm scared."

They were some of the truest words Madelyn had muttered since she'd arrived here.

Her words seemed to soften the chief. His shoulders relaxed and his voice sounded lower. "I know you're scared. I would be, too. I'm going to get to the bottom of this."

"Thank you, Chief. I can't tell you how much better that makes me feel."

His gaze caught hers. He gingerly touched her chin and tilted her head toward him. "You have a small cut on your temple."

As her skin came alive, she sucked in a breath. She reached for her wound and felt the blood there. In her rush of adrenaline, she hadn't even noticed.

After examining her one more minute, Zach opened his door. "Let's go inside and get you cleaned up before we get back to the crime scene. Hopefully, Tyler is already there and preserving the area."

He climbed out before she had the chance to argue. Madelyn scrambled out behind him, uncomfortable with being left alone, no matter how illogical it might be. When she stepped into Zach's house, she froze, expecting to feel fear again at the blood she'd seen last time she was here.

But Zach had cleaned it up after recording all the evidence. The place looked homey now.

"Make yourself comfortable," Zach said. "I'll be right back."

Madelyn lingered in the kitchen until he emerged from the back hallway, a first-aid kit in hand. He set it on the counter, pulled out some ointment and a Band-Aid.

"Should I tell you this is going to sting a little?"

"Understood." Despite that understanding, she still flinched as the medicine-drenched gauze hit her forehead.

"I tried to warn you."

She opened her eyes and sucked in a breath. She'd known Zach would be close, but she hadn't expected the whoosh of attraction at his nearness.

His face was near enough that she could see the flecks in his blue eyes. She spotted a wayward curl that had drifted onto his forehead. She caught a whiff of his woodsy cologne. Something about the combination made her feel off balance.

What would it be like to kiss him?

She jerked with surprise as soon as the thought entered her mind. Where had that come from? She had no business thinking like that. No business at all. She was writing an article that would destroy the man's life potentially. She had to get a grip, especially in light of her true intentions.

"Whoa. Everything okay?" His eyes narrowed in curiosity and concern.

Good. He thought her reaction was from the ointment. She'd let him continue to think that. The idea of him knowing her real thoughts seemed too horrifying.

"Just a little squeamish," she said.

"Almost done."

As he stretched the Band-Aid across her wound, she

closed her eyes—lest her thoughts get the best of her again. Finally, Zach patted it in place and stepped back.

She swallowed hard. "I don't think you have anything to worry about it. It's really just a scratch."

"It could have been so much worse."

As he pulled back, she forced her eyes open. Mistake. Zach's eyes were studying her, remaining on her long enough that she squirmed.

"I have a question for you," he started.

"Shoot."

"Is this yours?" He reached into his pocket and pulled out a slip of paper. He held it up, balanced between his index and middle fingers.

Her eyes widened when she saw her handwriting scribbled there. Her words. His information. The slip of paper Madelyn had lost. Her cheeks burned. "You caught me."

He waited, not saying anything.

"I have a terrible memory, so I write down a lot. Eva Rogers, 56 years old, degree from the local community college, two sons and three granddaughters. Mayor Bill Alan. 58 years old. Considered a real-estate mogul. Self-taught— or self-made, as he says. Used money from his inheritance to start buying up properties in the area when they were still cheap. Should I go on?"

Zach stared at her a moment, as if trying to gauge the truth in her words. Had he bought it? Her words were partially the truth. She liked to do her research and have her facts straight. She *had* researched other people in town before she came. But she'd especially researched Zach. She didn't have to tell him that, though.

"But you wrote my information down?" he asked.

She shrugged. "I wrote down material about everyone. I just happened to drop yours."

He finally nodded, as if he accepted her answer. "I see."

"I know it seems strange," she offered feebly.

"We all have our methods." He nodded toward the door. "Anyway, we need to go look at your apartment now. See if any evidence was left behind after those bullets went flying."

She let out the breath she'd been holding. He'd bought it. Thank goodness.

But just as quickly as she relaxed, she remembered her apartment—the overturned couches and tables and broken dishes. The gunshot had temporarily taken that out of her mind. There was still a lot on the line here.

It was too soon to start feeling safe.

EIGHT

Zach and Tyler worked the scene of the shooting, as well as the breaking and entering at Madelyn's apartment.

Three bullets had been fired. One was embedded in the outside wall of Madelyn's apartment, only inches from where she'd exited her apartment.

"Strangest case I've ever seen." Tyler paused and observed the scene in the parking lot, shaking his head.

The officer was in his midtwenties. He was tall with tanned skin and a full head of dark hair. The man was good-looking and he knew it. He'd grown up in the town, and people here loved him. He'd become somewhat of a local celebrity several years ago when he'd made a national calendar featuring the hottest law enforcement officers on the East Coast.

Zach had been surprised when he'd started to actually like Tyler. He wasn't the sharpest officer Zach had ever met, but he was faithful. Tyler had told Zach when he'd arrived in town that he had no desire to be chief, that he didn't want that responsibility. The two seemed to work well together.

The few misdemeanors they'd had to handle since Zach arrived had been simple. But with this surge in crime over the past few days, Zach found himself longing for someone more experienced than Tyler as his lone officer. He supposed this crime spree would prove what Tyler was really made of.

"Someone wasn't trying to steal anything. I'm not even convinced they're trying to kill Madelyn. I think someone wants to scare her," Zach said.

"Why would someone want to scare her?" Tyler scratched his head, his eyes concealed by sunglasses even though the sun was below the edge of the buildings.

"That's what we need to figure out."

"Maybe she's hiding something."

Zach glanced around. A good-sized crowd had gathered around the area. Crime-scene tape had been strung along the perimeter, blocking off the area to any passersby. This shooting spree would be the talk of the town, and how Zach handled it would set a precedent for the rest of his time here in Waterman's Reach.

Zach wasn't intimidated. He knew how to handle himself in stressful situations. He only hated how unsettled all of this left him feeling.

His gaze traveled across the parking lot. Madelyn sat on a nearby bench, stoically watching everything as it happened. The woman appeared shell-shocked, and Zach couldn't blame her. She'd been through a lot today. And yesterday for that matter. And the day before.

Maybe she's hiding something.

Tyler had voiced the idea out loud, but Zach had wondered that himself plenty of times. What did Madelyn know that she wasn't sharing?

Out of the corner of his eye, he saw Levi Watson, the town's former chief, approaching him. Great. This was just what Zach needed. The man always tried to tell Zach how he would handle things, and it extended to everything from parking violations to the hours Zach kept.

Levi Watson was large, all the way from his shoulders to his oversized stomach. He still had a shock of black hair that contrasted with his ruddy, wrinkled face. Around those he liked, the man was jolly and full of goodwill. But for those not on Levi's favorable side, his stormy demeanor was sure to bring on a headache. He liked to make things difficult for those who didn't support him or his ideas.

"I heard we had a shooting." Levi surveyed the scene around him, raising his nose with disdain. He paused from his negative demeanor for long enough to wave at one of his friends who passed by.

Zach nodded. "That's correct."

"In my twenty-three years as chief, we only had one shooting, and that was out at someone's home in a domestic dispute. Never in downtown."

"Someone decided that today would be the day to challenge that record." Zach had learned to let what Chief Watson said roll off his back. The man was looking for a reason to fuss and to prove Zach was incompetent. He'd wanted his nephew Tyler to get the job.

"Any idea who's responsible?" Levi continued.

"At this point, no. We're still tracking some leads."

He nodded, a little too smugly. Somehow, in Levi's mind, all of this was Zach's fault. "If you need my assistance, let me know. I'd be happy to step in."

"I appreciate the offer. Now, if you don't mind, I should get back to work." Zach nodded toward the scene. Tyler was talking to the crowd, trying to ease their fears. Meanwhile, Zach needed to get these bullets in for ballistics testing. He was curious to know if they matched the one that was fired at him in the woods.

"Of course."

With that, Zach approached Madelyn. There was no need for her to sit out here any longer. They were almost ready to wrap up and go back to the office.

"Your place is clear if you want to go back up," he told her. "We've done our best to help straighten it up, and

Tyler told the mayor what had happened, so he's aware of the situation."

She nodded weakly, uncrossing her legs and straightening. "I appreciate that."

Something about the way she said the words led him to believe that she was scared but trying to be tough. Zach could admire that. It was a sign of strength to be able to push past fears.

"I also had Tyler change the locks," Zach continued. "There was no sign of forced entry, which made us wonder if somehow the person who broke in had a key to the place."

"Maybe a friend of Mayor Alan's? Or maybe they rented it before and made a copy?"

"We're hoping to figure that out." Zach stepped closer. "If it makes you feel better, there are a couple of bed-and-breakfasts in town. I'm sure we could house you at one of those if you'd be more comfortable."

Madelyn stood, slowly shaking her head. She stared at the house and frowned again. "You don't have to do that. I'll be careful."

"These threats are only escalating. If, at any time, you feel like you're in danger, call me and I'll be here. Okay?" He meant it. He felt a duty to keep an eye on her. This was his town, she was a guest here and she didn't deserve to be terrorized like this.

Her eyes widened with some unreadable emotion at his offer. The sentiment behind her reaction looked like more than fear, but he couldn't identify it exactly.

Finally, she smiled, though the action looked stiff and forced. "I will. I promise."

The truth remained that staying by herself was the last thing that Madelyn wanted. She wanted to run from this place, from this town, from Zach Davis and the way he made her feel so safe and protected. He made her emotions feel bipolar. In one moment, she felt secure with him. The next moment, she thought for sure her life was in danger when he was close.

But she couldn't run. This could be her big break. This was her chance to prove to Paula that she had a career in journalism. This was her chance to make an impact in the world by ensuring that justice was served. She was disappointed in herself that she hadn't had more time to investigate. At this point, she'd mostly been running for her life and questioning her own assumptions.

She'd never make it as a reporter if she kept letting her emotions take control. Maybe deep down inside, Zach was a nice guy who'd made some bad choices. That didn't mean he shouldn't have consequences for his actions.

Right now Madelyn sat in bed with her knees pulled to her chest. She'd turned the light off—begrudgingly, at that—and now she sat in the dark. A sliver of light crept in through the window, probably from one of the streetlights outside.

Every little creak made her jump. Every shadow from a passing vehicle made the air leave her lungs. Her imagination was working overtime as she pictured the man who'd shown up on her first day here showing up again. Making good on his promise. Sending her another message about how she wasn't welcome in this town.

She heard another creak, and her chest muscles tightened.

Was it the building settling? Buildings did that, right? That's what she'd always heard.

Or was someone in the apartment?

Her throat went dry at the thought of someone else invading her space. In here, there was no one to hear her scream. No one was living downstairs right now, and she hadn't seen anyone in either of the houses beside her. Her impression was that they were summer homes for retired couples who lived in Florida during the winter.

No, someone could kill her up here and her body wouldn't be discovered for hours. Days maybe. Until maybe Eva or Zach caught wind that she was gone, even though her car was still outside.

Every time she closed her eyes, she felt the whiz of the bullet sweeping by her. She felt Zach's strong arms covering her. She remembered her absolute fear.

If someone was trying to scare her, he was doing a good job.

Another squeak sounded. Was it closer this time? Maybe the hallway?

She pulled the covers up higher, hating the fact that she felt like a little girl. Only, when she was a little girl, she'd had her daddy to protect her. What she wouldn't give to have him in her life now. She missed him and her mom every day.

But they weren't here anymore, so she had to act like the grown woman she was.

How many creaks would it take before she took action? She couldn't just sit here and wait to be a victim.

Her limbs trembled as she stood from her bed. She could hardly breathe. But she needed to prove to herself that this duplex was safe.

She pulled on her robe and grabbed the knife she'd put on her nightstand. It had been the only weapon she'd been able to find. At the last minute, she slipped her cell phone into her pocket.

She'd call Zach if she had to. But she didn't want to be the woman who cried wolf when there was really no danger. Her paranoia may be getting the best of her.

After all, before she'd gone to bed, she'd checked all of the doors and even the windows. Zach had even had Tyler change the front lock for her. So why didn't she feel secure?

Maybe she should have taken Zach's suggestion and stayed at a bed-and-breakfast for the evening. But would she be safe there even? Was there anywhere she'd be safe? Madelyn wasn't sure.

After drawing in a deep breath, she stepped out of the bedroom. Her gaze flickered around the hallway. She expected to see a figure lurking in the shadows. But the area was empty.

What had that noise been?

Madelyn would never know if she stayed here. She slowly stepped forward, remaining close to the wall and on alert. She felt hypersensitive as survival instinct kicked in.

A pattering sounded in the distance. Madelyn threw herself against the wall, nearly clawing into the plaster. Her heart pounded in her ears as fear began to take control.

She flung her head toward the sound, desperate for answers. The balcony, she realized. That was where the noise had come from. As she eased into the living room, she stared at the French doors, waiting for a sign of what was happening.

She nearly laughed when she saw the plants on the balcony swaying, along with an outside curtain.

It was just the wind, she realized. The breeze from the bay had scattered sand onto the glass windowpanes. The curtain flapped against the glass.

The sound was louder than she'd imagined. But at least Madelyn could rest easy now. All she'd been hearing was an approaching storm.

With slow steps she started back to her room. The events of the past couple of days were playing with her mind and making her hear things that weren't there. How much longer would she live in paranoia like this?

She rounded the corner toward the hallway when someone lunged from the darkness. The knife flew from her hand as strong arms pinned her in place.

Madelyn gasped, the air leaving her lungs as her body slammed into the wall. Pain throbbed in her head, but she ignored it.

A man wearing all black stared back at her. All Madelyn could see were his eyes, and they were pools of darkness.

Her heartbeat ratcheted out of control at the sight. They were the eyes of a killer, she realized. Fear tried to paralyze her at the thought.

"You have no place here," the man grumbled. "You only want to start trouble."

Trouble? The only person who might think that was Zach. There was no one else here she could start trouble with.

Was Zach behind all of this? She'd tried to warn herself, to remember that he could be vile beneath his nice-guy exterior. Why hadn't she listened to her instincts?

"I...I don't want to start trouble," she whispered.

He slammed her into the wall again. "Stop lying! I know who you are."

Her head ached with even more intensity and the room spun. His grip on her arms was so strong that she knew she couldn't get away.

"Stop investigating," he growled. His hand went to her throat and he pressed on it.

She couldn't breathe. She let out a feeble cry as she realized that the man was going to kill her.

NINE

Zach worked on his police report in his car, still unable to get over everything that had happened in this small, sleepy town over the past couple of days. He looked out the window and checked the moon.

No, it wasn't full. He'd seen his fair share of people acting crazy when the moon was full and bright in the sky.

So what could he blame the strange events on? Something was going on in this town. Most likely it involved Madelyn Sawyer. He just couldn't imagine what the pretty lady might have gotten herself caught up in.

He lowered his window slightly, wanting to hear the waves crashing in the distance. There was something calming about the sound, and he could use some calm right about now.

Lord, what's going on? Are You trying to show me something?

Just as he muttered a mental *amen*, he heard something shatter in the distance.

That had come from Madelyn's place.

He darted from his vehicle toward the duplex. His muscles strained as he sprinted, but he still couldn't move fast enough. He took the stairs by two and didn't bother to knock. He had the extra key and had intended on giving it to Mayor Alan in the morning.

He barged into her apartment with his gun drawn. Silence greeted him and as each second ticked past, his muscles tightened even more.

He scanned the dark apartment, searching for a sign of trouble.

Out of the corner of his eyes, he saw a figure running toward the balcony. That wasn't Madelyn. Someone had been in here with her.

Protectiveness surged through him.

The figure jumped over the balcony. Instinct told him to follow the man, but he had to check on Madelyn first. He feared the worst.

Darting through the house, he searched for her. She wasn't in the kitchen or the living room. Finally he spotted her in the corner of the hallway. She crouched on the floor, holding her throat.

He knelt beside her and quickly checked for any obvious injuries. He saw none. "Are you okay?"

With her eyes squeezed with fear, she pointed toward the balcony. "Go," she whispered.

His heart was pulled in two different directions. "Are you sure?"

"Absolutely."

After a moment of hesitation, he shot down the stairs. This was his chance to catch this guy, and he didn't want to miss it.

He dashed to the beach side of the building in time to see the man head for the water. The man limped; he'd probably injured himself when he'd hurdled the balcony railing. Zach hoped that would work to his advantage.

Zach pounded across the sand, his muscles burning with each step. The man had a head start. But Zach was determined to catch him and put an end to this once and for all.

Suddenly, the man stopped. He crouched a moment before turning toward Zach and flinging something from his hand.

Sand.

The specks invaded Zach's eyes, temporarily blinding him. He bent over, trying to clear his vision before the man slipped away.

It was no use. The sand wasn't coming out any time soon.

Despite that, Zach pulled his eyes open and pushed forward. Everything around him was fuzzy and hazy. He could barely make out the man running again in the distance.

He didn't want to lose him. Not when he was so close.

The man reached the shoreline and jumped into a waiting boat. The driver of the watercraft sped off into the distance, taking the suspect with him.

He'd lost him, Zach realized. The sand in his eyes had prevented him from even getting a good look at the man.

But he wasn't giving up yet.

This was nowhere near over.

From her perch on the balcony, Madelyn saw Zach walking back toward the house, and she rushed downstairs to meet him. His eyes were puffy and watery, not to mention the fact that he was blinking uncontrollably.

"Are you okay? What happened?" Instinctively, Madelyn's hands went to his arm. She'd only gone outside onto the balcony a moment earlier and hadn't seen everything play out. What had the man done to him?

"I just need a sink," he muttered.

Madelyn didn't ask any questions. Not now.

Instead, she helped him upstairs to the kitchen and watched as he ran water over his eyes. When he was done, she handed him a kitchen towel and he blotted his face.

"I can't say that's ever happened to me before," he mumbled, still leaning over the sink, his hands near his eyes.

"What happened?"

"He threw sand in my eyes. A simple yet effective deterrent."

Concern echoed through her. That had to hurt. "Are you okay?"

"Yeah. He got away. There was a boat waiting by the pier for him."

She frowned. "Did you get a good look at him?"

"Unfortunately, no. How about you?" He turned and leaned against the sink, running his index fingers under his eyes.

Madelyn shook her head. "No, he jumped out from behind me. And he was wearing a mask."

Zach's gaze fastened on hers, studying her as he had several times since they'd met. "Are you okay?"

She wrapped her arms over her chest, a tremble rushing through her. She'd thought she was going to die. Her jaw hurt. Her head hurt. Her pride hurt for that matter.

"Yeah, I'm fine," she said. "Thanks to you. Again. How'd you get here so quickly? I didn't even call."

"I decided to stay outside in the car, just in case." He shrugged like it was no big deal.

Her cheeks flushed. In that moment, however quick, she didn't feel alone. Someone had been watching out for her. The realization brought her a brief yet immense comfort. "That was nice of you."

"Just doing my job," he clarified, raising his chin.

"Of course," she said quickly, not wanting him to get the wrong impression. Her cheeks heated. Thankfully, Zach didn't seem to notice, and he pressed ahead.

"Did the man say anything? Give you any clue about who he was or why he was here?"

Madelyn shook her head. "Nothing."

"He must have come in from the other side of the building because I had my eye on the front door all night."

Zach walked to the balcony and looked down. "I suppose it would possible for someone to scale the side of the house near the mounted water hose. If he was agile enough, he may be able to reach the balcony and climb up here. Still, the doors were locked, correct?"

She nodded, mentally running through her routine this evening. "I checked them again before I went to sleep."

"It just doesn't make sense. Of course, Tyler didn't change these locks, only the front." He rubbed his neck. "Regardless of that, I don't think you should stay here, not until we know how this guy is getting in and out. I don't think he'll come back tonight, but it seems like he's becoming more aggressive and that makes me nervous."

"It's the middle of the night. Where am I supposed to go?" Again, that mental reminder of how alone she was in the world almost seemed to overwhelm her. Though she had no one to hold her back from achieving her dreams, she also had no one to hold her hand on the hard days. The thought made her feel hollow inside.

"Nowhere tonight. You're right—it's too late. If you're comfortable with it, I'll stay on your couch. Otherwise I can wait in my car, but I'd feel better if I were closer."

He's just doing his job, Madelyn reminded herself. He wasn't showing her any special care or attention. It would be best if she kept that at the forefront of her thoughts. "If you wouldn't mind, I'd appreciate it."

"Of course."

She wandered to the closet, grabbed a blanket and a pillow, and placed them on the sofa. She suddenly felt self-conscious, unsure if she should make polite conversation or just leave him alone.

She slowly lowered herself into the chair across from him and hugged a pillow to her chest. Just a moment of talking couldn't hurt anything. "I'm crazy for staying in Waterman's Reach, aren't I?"

She wasn't sure where the moment of honesty had come from. Maybe she just needed someone to talk to, someone besides Paula. Paula never seemed to hear what she said; she only heard what she wanted.

"Probably. Why *are* you staying here?" He sat across from her and leaned back on the couch as if he was exhausted.

"I have a job to do. I want to make my editor happy. I don't want to be intimated into doing something." All of those reasons were true. She wasn't sure which took first priority, though.

He nodded slowly. "Makes sense."

Madelyn's throat tightened. She realized she could easily pour everything out to Zach, and she couldn't risk that. Instead, she stood. "How about if I fix you some water? Tea?"

"Just water sounds great. Thank you."

She hurried into the kitchen and grabbed a bottle from the refrigerator. The mayor had left them for her, as well as several other convenience items like snack-sized packages of crackers and cereal.

"You really do need to get some rest," she said, trying to keep the conversation in safe territory. "You don't want to make yourself sick."

"I'll be okay. But thank you."

She pressed her lips together, realizing she'd sounded like her mom. Her mom in this situation, however, would have had pie ready, clean towels laid out and little mints to leave on his pillow.

"Seriously, you seem to be working nonstop since I've been here," Madelyn said. "I know this is a small town and all, but have they ever considered hiring anyone else to help you?"

"You mean besides Tyler?"

She handed him his water bottle, noting that he'd unbuttoned the top of his shirt. Why did seeing him look so relaxed send a surge of attraction through her? She had to nix these feelings, especially considering the reason she was here. There was no room for real feelings to develop. "Yes, besides Tyler."

He twisted the top off and took a long sip. "Small-town departments don't usually have this much excitement. I'm hoping things will calm down soon."

As she sat down, she pulled her legs under her and leaned into the chair. "Like when I leave?"

"I didn't say that."

"You didn't have to." She knew the truth, even if she didn't like it.

He leaned back and studied her a moment. "So, if you weren't here doing an article with a crazy person after you, what would you think of this town?"

Her thoughts wandered a moment. She only ever went to new places for articles. Otherwise, she'd just be taking a vacation alone, which didn't sound like fun. She shrugged. "I'd think it was nice."

"Nice?" His eyebrows shot up in surprise. "That's awfully generic."

She let out a self-conscious laugh. "Well, traveling by myself isn't always a blast."

"Okay, say you had someone with you. Then what would you think?"

She imagined it a moment before slowly nodding. The thought was so bittersweet, a longing she tried to bury. "I would like it. Spending some time on the beach, a carriage ride, shopping, eating at these restaurants. I heard there are some great waterside towns to explore. Maybe by kayak."

"By kayak?" He raised his eyebrows.

She nodded. "Yeah, I've always wanted to try. Somewhere placid, you know? But not too swampy. I think the water in the bay and the little creeks around it would be perfect."

"You're right. It's ideal for paddling out."

For a moment she imagined herself being with Zach on her journey. Pausing to have a picnic on the beach. Stealing some pictures together in between their travel locations.

The thought pleased her so much that she found herself flushing. Thank goodness he couldn't read her thoughts. That would just be too humiliating.

Sure, the man had saved her life a few times. But that didn't mean he was a good guy or her knight in shining armor. She had to stop forgetting that.

Suddenly, Madelyn stood, knowing she was treading dangerous waters here. She needed some distance from Zach. "I should let you get some rest."

He nodded slowly, almost reluctantly. "It was good chatting, Madelyn."

"Good night, then. And thank you again."

As she turned to leave, Zach grabbed her wrist. At once, she imagined herself in his arms, wrapped in his embrace.

Fire spread through her skin at his touch.

"Are you sure you're okay, Madelyn?" he asked her.

She nodded, nearly unable to breathe as she stared into his intense gaze. "I promise—I'm fine."

But she'd be even better when she was farther away from Zach Davis. Because when she was around him, either her heart was in danger or her life.

TEN

Madelyn raised her face to the breeze as the boat whipped through Mockhorn Bay the next morning.

She'd chartered the watercraft to take her on a tour this morning. She had to somehow keep up the appearance that she was writing a travel piece on Waterman's Reach. That meant doing things like exploring the bay and other activities that tourists might find interesting.

Captain Ernie had taken her on a tour of the barrier islands that stretched across what locals called the seaside, which really meant the ocean side, of the peninsula. Once inhabited, the islands were now abandoned and subject to the weather. The landmasses were doing what they were meant to do: protect the coastline. They were beautiful and untouched.

The perfect place for crimes to be committed.

Madelyn shook her head. Now where had that thought come from? Too many things had happened lately, and it had made her think that crime was waiting around every corner, she supposed.

She'd been strangely disappointed this morning when she'd gotten up and found that Zach was gone. She'd discovered the blanket neatly folded on the couch and the pillow atop it.

It was silly, really. Why should it matter if he was there or not? She didn't even trust the man.

But if that were true why had she agreed to let him sleep on her couch?

Her conflicting thoughts toyed with her emotions. Either the man was honorable or he wasn't. She had to stop wafting back and forth.

But his presence last night had calmed her down. She'd actually gotten some rest, a fact that surprised her.

Against her better instincts, she smiled. His image filled her mind. He was certainly handsome. But his attractiveness came from more than his good looks. He was proving himself to be respectable.

Before she'd met him, he'd just been a character: a combination of facts and things she'd read in articles. Now that she was here and getting to know him, he was becoming real. He had stories to tell and a past he'd lived and a future ahead of him.

And that made everything more complicated.

Madelyn looked out over the crystal-blue water, which looked picture-perfect from the gentle waves all the way up to the seagulls squawking overhead.

"I heard you've had some trouble since you've been in town," Captain Ernie said.

She turned to him, surprise lighting her eyes.

The captain shrugged. "It's a small town. Word gets around quickly."

Finally, she nodded. Why deny it? People would find out eventually. "Maybe someone doesn't want my article written about Waterman's Reach. It's the only thing I can think of."

"Now what sense would that make? It's a travel article. Who wouldn't want to increase tourism in the area?"

Madelyn had thought about it. On the surface that made sense. But things were rarely that simple.

"There are people who resist change," Madelyn said over the motor. "They like things the way they are and the way they've always been. Maybe someone doesn't want this town to change."

Ernie waved his hand in the air. "I just can't see it. A lot of people's livelihoods depend on this town prospering. The fishing industry just isn't enough anymore. After the factory on the outskirts of town closed, it's really limited the number of jobs in this area."

"Except for the fishermen. They seem to be doing just fine without any tourists coming here. As long as their livelihoods are secure, maybe the rest of the town doesn't matter. Is there anyone who's been really resisting the change?"

Ernie shook his head. "No. No one. I just hope Chief Davis can get a handle on this. Chief Watson wouldn't have stood for this."

Now that was an interesting comment. "Really? You don't think Chief Davis is doing a good job? Earlier you made it sound like you did."

Ernie's eyes widened with surprise. Had the man said more than he'd wanted? That's how it appeared.

"No, of course not." He let out a weak laugh. "I think some people like to test the limits of the new guy in town, you know? Chief Watson was such a fixture around here. Like you said, some people don't like change. They don't like it one bit."

Madelyn chewed on his words a moment.

Captain Ernie slowed down, shifting the attention to the water around them. "I suppose they've already told you about the fishing industry here in town?"

Madelyn shook her head. "Only that it's booming."

"You should tag along with one of the fishermen sometime. It's pretty amazing the work they do. They know how to plant the oysters in beds where they'll prosper. They have to know exactly when to harvest them and how many they can harvest. And you're here in town at just the right time. It's oyster season."

"Lucky me," she said. The oyster industry really had nothing to do with her article, though she was sure it might be interesting to some people.

Just then, she felt something shift beneath her. The entire boat stopped. Then the motor died.

In the middle of the bay.

Zach looked up from his desk at the sound of someone knocking at the door. His friend Chris Kent stood there. Chris was a coastguardsman that Zach had become friends with during Zach's time as sheriff over in Smuggler's Cove. The man was five foot ten, stocky and dedicated. The two of them got together for coffee every couple of weeks, and Zach had asked him to come by today.

"Thanks for coming," Zach said.

"I heard you've been busy here." Chris shut the door and sat across from Zach. His frame took up most of the chair.

"Unfortunately, something messed up is going on here in Waterman's Reach, and I wanted to get your input."

He'd called his friend last night because he was one of the few people Zach trusted completely. Zach recounted to him now everything that had happened over the past several days.

"What do you think this is about?" Chris asked.

Zach let out a long breath. "That's the question of the hour. This somehow ties in with the new reporter in town."

"Did you look into her background?" Chris leaned back in the chair, laid-back and acting like they were talking about Fantasy Football or something else that wasn't life threatening. It was because he dealt with issues like these every day. He'd learned how to cope with the stresses of small-town crime.

"I did look into her background, and she seems squeaky-

clean, which brings me back to why I asked you to come."
Though the only other person in the office was Lynn, Zach
lowered his voice. "I wonder if someone has become aware
that I've asked you to keep an eye on our coast."

Chris stared in the distance for a moment before shaking
his head. "Not on my end. I haven't mentioned it to anyone,
so all of my colleagues simply think I'm doing my job. Did
you tell anyone else here about your concerns?"

Zach shook his head. He'd kept his quest silent so he
wouldn't tip anyone off. He suspected that drugs were being
brought into the country through the secluded coastline off
the barrier islands. He couldn't prove it—but he was trying.

He felt certain the drugs used up in the Baltimore drug
bust could be traced back to this coastline and this town.

"No, I haven't trusted this information to anyone else."

"Not even Tyler?"

"Not even Tyler. The fewer people who know, the better."

"I don't blame you for staying quiet. News like that
would be the talk of the town."

"So there's been nothing out of the ordinary out there
lately?" All Zach needed was one lead to give him hope.
But that one lead was proving harder to come by than he
would like to think.

Chris shook his head. "We had that drug bust out there
about two months ago. Huge shipment of marijuana. But it
wasn't the heroin you're looking for. Those barrier islands
are like a playground for anyone wanting to be secretive.
It's one of the most underdeveloped coastlines on the East
Coast. But that makes catching people even harder. We
patrol the waters, but there are a lot of waters to patrol and
we can't be everywhere at once."

Zach thought about his words for moment, leaning back
in his chair as his mind raced. "If not on one of those con-

tainer ships, how are they getting these drugs into this part of the country?"

"If it is on one of the container ships, there's not much of a chance that we'll find them. Border patrol's dogs will sniff out the shipments, but they don't find everything."

"I know these drugs are coming out of Waterman's Reach."

"You could very well be right. But good luck proving it. I'll continue to keep my eyes open."

Zach reached out to shake his hand. "I appreciate it. Thank you."

Zach remained in his chair after Chris left, chewing on their conversation. He'd hoped for more. But he had to learn to be patient. He'd never find any answers if he wasn't.

The crime spree in town had lessened the amount of time he had to look into the drugs anyway.

As soon as Chris left, Zach's phone rang. It was a man named Caleb Feldman from the state crime lab.

"I was going through your new evidence. The report says that there are three bullets. However, only two came in as evidence."

"What are you talking about? That's impossible."

"I'm just telling you what I'm looking at right now. One of the state police officers brought everything in to the lab for us to test. But, since there was a discrepancy, I wanted to let you know."

"I'll see what I can find out."

"In other news, these bullets match the one you sent me earlier—the one imbedded in the tree."

So the man Zach had chased through the woods was the driver of the white truck.

"It appears to be from a standard-issue Glock, not a rifle, as it might have been had it been a hunter out there in the woods."

"Interesting."

"One more thing," Caleb said. "That blood you sent in? It was from a pig."

Zach leaned back in his chair and raised his eyebrows. He bounced a pencil on his desk calendar as he processed that. "A pig?"

"You can buy pig's blood at Asian markets and other places. It's used to make blood pudding or blood sausages, so it's pretty easy to obtain."

"Good to know."

"I don't know what's going on, but does that help?"

Zach continued to bounce the pencil as he mulled over the new information. Someone wanted to make Zach look like he was a bad guy. Was this person making it a point to do it in front of Madelyn? She'd been the only one to see it.

But that didn't make sense. No one could have anticipated that Madelyn would swing by his house that day.

Only two people knew about the ride along—the mayor and Eva. What if one of them had left the door to his house open, knowing he'd be called in to check it out? Then Madelyn would see the blood there. He didn't want to believe that either of those people would be behind the acts, though.

The only other option seemed to be that someone was playing mind games with Zach. Maybe someone was trying to distract him from the other issues going on in the area, to keep him busy with mindless cases so he'd miss something bigger.

"Zach?" Caleb repeated.

"Sorry. Yes, that information does help. Thank you for pushing this ahead of your other projects. We have a situation going on here in town, and it's very timely."

"No problem, man."

With the prevalence of the internet, Zach knew it would be nearly impossible to track down who in town had purchased pig's blood. It would end up being a colossal waste of time. Perhaps another distraction so he'd miss something else.

His gut told him that the answers rested with Madelyn. She may not even realize it, but what if all of this linked back to her somehow? Maybe he needed to dig deeper into her background.

"Thanks again. I'll look into that third bullet and see what I can find out."

Zach hung up and leaned back in his chair. What had happened to the third bullet? Tyler had helped him log the evidence. He, Tyler and the state trooper were the only ones who'd handled the information. So what had happened?

At that moment, a shadow appeared in his doorway. Tyler. Just the man he wanted to see. He must have returned from patrol.

"Any updates on the shooting yesterday?" Tyler asked.

"A bullet's missing. Know anything about it?"

Tyler gawked. "That's impossible. I collected those bullets myself."

"Did anyone else come in contact with them?"

Tyler shook his head. "No, no one."

"Was there anyone else lurking around as you were collecting the evidence?" Zack asked.

"No one. Except the Mayor. He stopped by, just for a few minutes."

"Mayor Alan?"

Tyler nodded. "I don't know what happened to that bullet, Chief. But I know I collected and bagged three of them."

That thought gnawed at Zach's gut. He prayed that the mayor wasn't involved in all of this. Because, if he was, then Zach wasn't sure who he could trust.

"We're taking on water," Captain Ernie said.

Madelyn stared at the liquid that poured in from the back

of the watercraft. It was coming in fast and already puddled at her feet. Her heart raced at the sight of it.

How had this happened? It just didn't make sense. "What's going on?"

Ernie stomped to the back of the boat and pulled the hatch off the engine. Steam shot out from inside. "Looks like a cooling system leak. Right before the engine shut down, the end cap burst and it caused the hull to split."

"What does all of that mean?" To Madelyn, he might as well have been speaking another language.

"It means this boat is of no use to us anymore."

"Can we make it to land?" She sounded breathless, even to her own ears.

Ernie grimaced. "It's doubtful. We're going to go under."

Her back muscles tightened as she glanced around. The nearest land she spotted was a barrier island that appeared to be at least a half a mile away. In between there were marsh grasses and oyster beds.

She shuddered at the thought of trudging through the water, or swimming against currents over her head, in order to reach safety. Even worse, she spotted dark clouds in the distance. Was a storm coming their way?

Ernie picked up his radio and pressed the button. Nothing happened. He tried again.

There was still no response.

Ernie tapped it with the palm of his hand. "This radio worked yesterday. Something's wrong with it now."

Madelyn knew what that meant: no Mayday calls.

And that couldn't be a coincidence. Someone had sabotaged the boat. Someone knew she was going on it today and wanted her to sink out here. This nightmare was never going to end, was it?

"I can use my cell phone," Madelyn said.

"Good luck getting a signal out here."

She stared at her screen. Sure enough—they were out of range.

Captain Ernie threw her a life preserver. "Put this on."

Madelyn's hands trembled as she pulled the bulky orange vest on and fastened the straps.

"You don't want to walk through those marshes," Ernie said, nodding toward a thick expanse of grass. "We're going to have to swim."

"Why can't we walk through the marshes?" It would keep them out of the chilly water and keep their body temperature more level. That made sense to Madelyn.

"There are still land mines there left over from when the government used this as a test area for their bombs. We can't take that chance."

Madelyn's stomach dropped.

She glanced toward the barrier island. There was a visible divider where the bay met the ocean. Angry waves crashed there, signaling waters that weren't always tranquil. Based on the force of those waves, Madelyn knew it was going to be dangerous trying to get to that island. She'd be fighting the strong current, and she'd never been the best swimmer.

"We have to make it to that island. The life jacket will keep you afloat. Okay?" Captain Ernie said.

Madelyn nodded. With the captain's guidance, she jumped into the frigid water.

She forced her arms to move. Slowly, surely, she got closer to the island in the distance. Captain Ernie, to his credit, stayed with her.

Her entire body shivered. She couldn't feel her fingers. And the clouds in the distance grew darker, came closer.

Finally her feet hit sand. She breathed a sigh of relief. The ground seemed to suction her feet, though, as she trudged toward the island in the distance. Finally, she fell on the shore there.

"We should try to find shelter," Ernie said. "It looks like we have a storm coming."

"There's shelter on this island?"

He shook his head. "There are trees on the far side. That's about as good as we're going to get."

Madelyn nodded, pulled herself to her feet and stared out at the island a moment.

She took in the vast expanse of land before her. There were no houses or other structures, only the rolling bay behind her, the mighty Atlantic in front of her and patches of marsh grass.

When they crested the slight sand dune, she saw a grove of trees on the far side. They were low and gnarled and huddled close as though they had to stick together or perish.

Ernie had told her earlier about the barrier islands and about how some boats were chartered as beach taxis for people who wanted to come and enjoy the sandy shores. Lodges and houses used to be located here, until people discovered just how treacherous the land was.

Finally, they reached the trees. She and Ernie huddled underneath one and braced themselves to wait this out until someone found them.

She picked up the conch shell at her feet and smiled despite the situation. She had a lot of memories of going to Ocean City, Maryland, for family vacations when she was a child. She and her dad would scour the beaches in the morning, trying to find all of the treasures they could. If they were really lucky, it would storm one day during their stay. She always found the best shells after the waves churned during storms coming from the east.

Those times with her family had felt like another lifetime ago. There was so little she had to hold on to from that part of her life. Not her family house. No heirlooms even. Not really. Her parents had both been teachers, so they didn't have much of value. Her mom hadn't even liked jewelry.

But it wasn't the material items that bothered her. It was the emotional connections. The support system. The safe net.

When she'd lost her parents and walked away from God, she'd lost all of that.

Was it too late to change? Did she even want to?

She wasn't sure where all the thoughts were coming from, but they were making her misty-eyed. She had to get a grip of her emotions.

It was all one cop's fault. If Darren Waters hadn't been gung ho about catching a thief, her parents would still be alive. He walked away from her tragedy unscathed.

Just like Zach had walked away from the Baltimore incident without consequence.

That shouldn't happen. When people messed up—whether out of carelessness or poor planning or apathy even—they should have penalties.

As a chilly wind blew over the land, she shivered again. The dark clouds were directly above them now, and Madelyn knew she needed to prepare for the worst. A storm had formed these islands; a storm could take them away.

ELEVEN

Why hadn't Madelyn returned yet? Zach had called her to no avail—the line had gone straight to voice mail each time. His impression was that she'd be back by now, and he'd wanted to convince her to move over to the bed-and-breakfast. He couldn't handle too many more sleepless nights of trying to stay outside her apartment to make sure she was okay.

Something didn't feel right in his gut. The woman always had her phone with her. She'd told him that Ernie was taking her out on a tour of the area's waterways today. Maybe she was out of range. Zach knew from firsthand experience that was entirely possible.

But he couldn't relax until he knew for sure. He grabbed his gear and headed over to the marina. Ernie Blankenship was the resident boat captain whom outsiders liked to use for charters. The man understood the rise and fall of the tides and knew how to traverse the waters and not get stuck on a sandbar, like so many outsiders tended to do.

Zach pulled up to the docks and saw that Madelyn's car was still there. He supposed that was a good sign. It meant she was most likely still out on the water. Given everything that had happened lately, he wanted to make sure.

Zach strode across the docks until he found Rod, the marina owner. He was sitting near a shack reserved for cleaning and scaling fish. The man was short and wrinkled. Zach had thought he was in his seventies when he first met him, but apparently he was only in his fifties. The sun and cigarettes had done a number on the man's skin, and his white hair only added to the effect.

"You seen Ernie?" Zach asked.

Rod shook his head and continued to clean a fish. "Not since he left this morning. You need to get up with him?"

Zach nodded, staring at the dark clouds in the distance. "I thought he'd be back by now."

"So did I. He told me he would just be out for a few hours. It's probably been closer to six, if I had to guess."

A wind brushed over the water, sending with it the scent of the sea. "There's a storm coming."

Rod put the fish down and propped his leg up on one of the pilings, leaning against his knee like he had all the time in the world. "He's out with that reporter."

Zach nodded. "I know. I'm afraid something is wrong, and I need you to take me out to check on them."

Rod looked at the dark clouds in the distance. "Storm's coming. It's going to get dangerous out there real quick."

"Even more reason to go now. What do you say? You know these waters better than anyone."

Zach didn't know the waterways around here well enough to navigate them, and he didn't want to take any chances, especially considering everything that had happened lately. The approaching storm only heightened his urgency.

A few minutes later, they boarded Rod's Tracker and were gliding across the water. Small whitecaps had formed and made the ride choppy. But that was nothing compared to how the water would be once the storm was upon them.

Zach scanned the expanse, looking for a sign of Ernie and Madelyn. A bad feeling churned in his gut.

Zach should have gone with Madelyn today. After everything that had happened so far, he should have known better. But he'd actually thought she might be safer out on the water than she was in Waterman's Reach. He'd been wrong.

"You have any idea where they went?" Rod asked over the roar of the engine, a toothpick dangling from his mouth.

"I just heard Ernie was taking her on a tour of the coast."

"I know where he generally takes people when they charter boats. We'll start there. I doubt he would have gone seaside. Not with the weather being iffy today."

Zach prayed that was true. The ocean waters would be so much more dangerous than the placid waters of the various bays and inlets between the peninsula and the barrier islands. With the storm in the distance, the waters were churning, anticipating the arrival of wind, thunder and lightning.

Miles of blue water passed around them while birds squawked, warning of the coming bad weather. In Zach's mind, they couldn't travel fast enough. Time was not on their side.

"Look, that's Ernie's boat!" Rod pointed to something bobbing in the water in the distance.

As they idled up closer to the boat, Zach was able to grab the side of it and pull the watercraft closer. He studied it a moment. The front appeared to be intact. But as his eyes traveled to the back, to the area around the engine, he saw the problem.

There was a crack in the hull, Zach realized. Between that and the lack of a Mayday call, he'd guess the boat had been sabotaged. There was no other reason for an incident like this to occur. Ernie was an experienced fisherman who knew how to take care of his watercraft.

But where were Madelyn and Ernie?

Alarm rose in him. His gaze scanned the water for any bobbing heads or flailing arms.

Nothing.

"Where's the closest barrier island?" Zach asked, turning against the wind to face the man.

"It's probably a half a mile out," Rod shouted, pointing at a landmass in the distance.

"We need to get there. Quickly." Just as Zach said the words, the first plop of rain hit him. The sky was completely dark now, and the waves were getting rockier.

Rod put the boat in gear and raced across the water. As he did, Zach searched the water for any sign of life. He didn't see anything or anyone.

He wasn't sure if that comforted him or not. Best-case scenario was that Ernie and Madelyn had made it to one of the barrier islands and were waiting until help arrived. Worst-case scenario…well, he couldn't go there.

Rod couldn't seem to go fast enough for his liking. But finally, the barrier islands came into view. The rain came down at a steady pace now, and thunder rumbled in the distance.

"Low tide will be here soon. If we're not careful, we'll be stuck on one of these sandbars," Rod warned.

"Let me just check the island."

Zach knew this was one of the local's favorites because of its raw beauty. It was a glorified sandbar, in reality. There was nothing here, though, except for a few trees on the opposite end. Searching it would be easy because of the unobstructed views. Once he crested the slight dune at the center of the island, he'd know whether or not Ernie and Madelyn were here.

Despite the rain that hammered his face, Zach finally reached the center of the island. He surveyed the shoreline, praying desperately that he would locate them. If Ernie and Madelyn weren't here, he didn't know where they might be.

His eyes widened when he spotted two people down the shoreline.

It was them! They were safe!

Thank You, Jesus.

Now Zach just had to figure out how to get them off this island before the storm unleashed all of its fury.

Madelyn huddled under the tree as rain came down hard. Not only was the downpour steady, but the drops were big and seemed to fall with unusual force. Out here on this island, the thunder sounded louder as it echoed across the water. The lightning seemed brighter as it reflected off the bay. The danger seemed even more real.

She and Ernie had been pacing the island for the past two hours, hoping for a sign of another boater. There had been several large tankers and container ships out in the ocean, but they had been too far away to notice them. All the other local boaters knew better than to be out here with an approaching storm.

Madelyn looked into the distance, hoping to see some sign of hope. She didn't even know what she was hoping for. But anything was better than staying here.

She blinked. Was she seeing things? Or was there a man walking down the shoreline toward her?

Could it be…Zach?

"Ernie! Look." She pointed, hoping desperately that she wasn't having some kind of hallucination.

He jerked his head toward the sight. "Well, what do you know…"

Madelyn took off in a run. She knew they didn't have much time and that their window of opportunity would quickly close for a safe departure from the island. Here, they had no real shelter from the rain and wind.

But on the boat, the bay could be a watery grave. The waves could certainly toss the boat, flip it and leave them at the mercy of nature.

Again.

But she'd take her chances out on the water.

As another thunderclap sounded overhead, she resisted a scream.

Zach grasped her arms when she reached him. His body looked rigid and on guard as his gaze soaked her in. "Are you okay?"

She nodded, touched by the worry in his gaze. "Now I am."

He waved at Ernie to join them before tugging her toward the shore. "Come on. Rod can get us back, but we don't have much time. This storm is going to be a doozy."

The wind worked against them, pushing them back and away from the shore. Every time the thunder rumbled, they all seemed to duck at the enormity of the sound. Lightning struck precariously close.

They weren't out of danger yet. Not even close.

Rod had remained in the boat, and he pulled up closer to them now. Zach had one hand on Madelyn as they waded through the chilly water. The waves lapped at them, soaking their pants and tugging on them.

Finally, Madelyn reached the boat. The way it bobbed back and forth would make it difficult to climb aboard.

"You've got this," Zach shouted over the wind.

Madelyn gripped the edge of the boat before putting her foot in Zach's outstretched palm. He boosted her inside, and she landed on the floor with a thud.

If Madelyn had been hoping to impress him, she'd utterly failed. Her hair clung to her face, her clothes were plastered to her body and any makeup was certainly long gone. Not to mention that she was the opposite of graceful.

None of that mattered, though. All that mattered was getting to safety.

Rod didn't waste any time. As soon as Zach and Ernie were aboard, he zoomed across the water. Whitecaps had already formed, and the ride was rocky, tossing everyone on board back and forth.

Lightning cracked in the distance, and thunder rolled overhead. The rain came down even harder. It was no longer a splattering of water. Buckets of moisture poured from the sky.

Madelyn sat in a seat at the back, holding on to the side for dear life. The rocky boat made her stomach feel uneasy and made her head spin.

She pulled a strand of wet hair from her eyes and glanced at Zach. He looked grim with his jaw set and his shoulders rigid. Madelyn noticed he sat close to her. Was that a coincidence, or was he purposely remaining near in case she started to topple overboard?

Cold-blooded killer, she reminded herself.

Why was it so difficult for her to remember that? When Madelyn was away from him, it came more easily. But when they were together, all of her suspicions seemed to disappear.

You're a terrible reporter, she told herself. *You've got to be tough, not so soft hearted.*

As a wave hit them, the boat nearly went airborne. Madelyn felt herself falling backward at the sudden motion. Zach's hand circled her waist, keeping her grounded.

Her pulse surged. Something about his touch made her tingle all over.

That wasn't good.

"It's only going to get worse," Zach said, leaning close enough that she could feel his breath on her ear. "We're still a good thirty minutes away, and the storm isn't fully on us yet."

She nodded, the sick feeling gurgling even stronger in her gut now. She knew this was serious, but his words had been a grim reminder of just how serious.

She tugged on her life jacket, knowing that such a simple device truly could save her life.

"I'm going to try and make it to Oyster," Rod yelled

over the hum of the boat and roar of the wind. "We're not going to make it to Waterman's Reach. There's no time. It's too dangerous."

Madelyn looked to the sky. She hoped they made it to safety in time.

She was halfway tempted to even pray.

But then she remembered all of her unanswered prayers. She couldn't handle any more.

TWELVE

Relief filled Zach as they reached the dock of the small fishing community of Oyster. It was one of the seaside towns that had once been a part of the booming seafood industry. Now it was only a few buildings and a couple of small fishing operations.

The sight was a welcomed reprieve.

Everyone on the boat was drenched when they arrived at the pier. The watercraft had nearly toppled several times. Lightning had struck precariously close, and everyone looked deathly pale from the turbulent waves.

"Watch your step!" Rod told everyone as the boat slammed into the pier.

With shaky steps, they all managed to climb onto the pier. Zach made sure everyone else was out before he pulled himself ashore. Madelyn had waited in the pouring rain for him, he realized.

The thought warmed him. She could have easily run ahead to get out of the weather.

He took her hand and pulled her toward the bait-and-tackle shop in the distance. Her hand trembled uncontrollably in his. She would get hypothermia if she wasn't careful.

The woman looked scared. She'd obviously been the target here—again.

We'd like to send you two free books from the series you are enjoying now. Your two books have a combined cover price of over $10 retail, but are yours to keep absolutely FREE! We'll even send you two wonderful surprise gifts. You can't lose!

Each of your FREE books is filled with joy, faith and traditional value and women open their hearts to each other and join together on a spiri journey.

GET 2 FREE BOOKS!

CLAIM NOW!
Return this card today to get 2 FREE Books and 2 FREE Bonus Gifts!

YES! Please send me the **2 FREE books** and **2 FREE gifts** for which I qualify. I understand that I am under no obligation to purchase anything further, as explained on the back of this card.

PLACE FREE GIFTS SEAL HERE

❑ I prefer the regular-print edition 153/353 IDL GKCF ❑ I prefer the larger-print edition 107/307 IDL GKCF

FIRST NAME

LAST NAME

ADDRESS

APT.#

CITY

STATE/PROV.

ZIP/POSTAL CODE

READER SERVICE—Here's how it works:

Accepting your 2 free Love Inspired® Suspense books and 2 free gifts (gifts valued at approximately $10.00) places you under no obligation to buy anything. You may keep the books and gifts and return the shipping statement marked "cancel." If you do not cancel, about a month later we'll send you 6 additional books and bill you just $4.99 each for the regular-print edition or $5.49 each for the larger-print edition in the U.S. or $5.49 each for the regular-print edition or $5.99 each for the larger-print edition in Canada. That is a savings of at least 17% off the cover price. It's quite a bargain! Shipping and handling is just 50¢ per book in the U.S. and 75¢ per book in Canada.* You may cancel at any time, but if you choose to continue, every month we'll send you 6 more books, which you may either purchase at the discount price or return to us and cancel your subscription. *Terms and prices subject to change without notice. Prices do not include applicable taxes. Sales tax applicable in N.Y. Canadian residents will be charged applicable taxes. Offer not valid in Quebec. Books received may not be as shown. All orders subject to approval. Credit or debit balances in a customer's account(s) may be offset by any other outstanding balance owed by or to the customer. Please allow 4 to 6 weeks for delivery. Offer available while quantities last.

▼ If offer card is missing write to: Reader Service, P.O. Box 1867, Buffalo, NY 14240-1867 or visit www.ReaderService.com ▼

BUSINESS REPLY MAIL
FIRST-CLASS MAIL   PERMIT NO. 717   BUFFALO, NY

POSTAGE WILL BE PAID BY ADDRESSEE

READER SERVICE
PO BOX 1867
BUFFALO NY 14240-9952

NO POSTAGE
NECESSARY
IF MAILED
IN THE
UNITED STATES

Zach wished he could do something to erase her terror. But fear was healthy, in this case. It would keep her vigilant and help keep her alive.

He was going to do everything in his power to ensure that. Probably the best thing he could do for her was to encourage her to go back home. She hadn't been experiencing these problems until she came here.

Finally, they reached the shop and stepped inside. Water dripped from them, dampening the floor. But it felt good to be out of the wind and rain.

"That was close," Ernie said, wiping water from his eyes.

"You can say that again," Zach said.

The owner had left a note on the door, saying he'd stepped out for lunch. Small-town businesses were known for being more trusting, but Zach wished someone was working here now. They needed blankets and warm drinks.

"My friend Will can give us a ride back in his truck," Rod said. "He lives right down the road."

"Why don't you and Ernie go ahead?" Zach said. "I'll wait here with Madelyn and see if Tyler can come pick us up."

Neither Rod nor Ernie argued. They were older, and they needed to get warm more than Zach or Madelyn did. Besides, Zach needed a minute alone to chat with Madelyn.

While Rod called his friend, Zach called Tyler. He didn't offer many details, just asked that he come right away. Madelyn was shivering uncontrollably beside him, and there was nothing Zach could do about it except encourage her to hang in.

The storm continued to rumble overhead, and rain pounded against the tin roof above. The sounds were almost a melody made by nature itself, a rhythmic drumbeat that set a creepy mood in the rustic space.

Around them were bare wood walls lined with fishing

hooks, tackle and fishing rods. The underlying scent of sea life lingered in the air, as well as the slight hint of oil.

After Ron and Ernie left, Zach turned toward Madelyn. She looked so unpresumptuous as she stood there. Her hair, normally perfectly styled, now formed wavy ringlets around her face. Her makeup had been washed off. Her clothing was wet and clung to her.

He'd never seen someone look so beautiful.

The thought surprised him and made him want to sock himself. He couldn't let his attraction to the woman grow. He had a mission here in Waterman's Reach, and he didn't want anything to distract him.

"Are you sure you're not hurt?" He resisted the impulse to reach out to her, even though she looked so alone standing there. He wished he had something to offer her—some coffee, a blanket, a change of clothes. But he had none of those things.

It was chilly in here, even chillier because they were wet. The lights flickered overhead as thunder rumbled again.

Madelyn nodded, although the action wasn't quite believable. "Yeah, I'm fine."

He stepped closer, despite his better instincts. "Madelyn, I don't think either of us can deny that..."

Her eyes widened.

"...someone is targeting you," he finished. "I know we've been through this before, but I keep hoping you'll remember something new."

Doubt—maybe even disappointment—flickered in her gaze for a moment before she finally shook her head. "You'd be the first person I told if I remembered something."

"Is there a reason why someone would follow you down from Maryland and try to harm you?"

She visibly shuddered. "I honestly can't think of any

enemies. I'm pretty private. I work and I go home. I'm not big on the social scene."

"Are you sure you haven't written any articles that angered anyone?"

She shook her head. "It's like I said, I write travel pieces."

"You've written a few that aren't just travel."

She flushed...more than flushed. She looked shocked for a moment. She stepped back and nervously pushed her hair away from her face. "You've researched me?"

"I'm just doing my job. If someone's trying to hurt you, it's my job to figure out why."

She swallowed hard and averted her gaze. She was getting ready to lie, he realized. But about what? And why?

"I've done a few other pieces," she said. "But nothing that would make anyone angry."

"You might be amazed at the things that upset some people."

"You think I'm naive?" A touch of defiance and a touch of hurt stained her gaze.

"I didn't say that. I'm just trying to explore all of the options here. Madelyn, I hate to tell you this, but there seems to be something about you and this town that doesn't mix. I want to help out Mayor Alan and the town in any way I can. The article you're writing sounds great. But it might be the best thing if you left."

An unreadable emotion sparked in her eyes. Indignation? Stubbornness? Determination? He couldn't be sure.

"I'm not leaving. I came here to do a job, and I'm going to do it."

"Even if your life is on the line?" He knew his voice had taken on a hard edge, but he needed to get through to her just how serious this was.

She raised her chin. "That's even more the reason to

stay. Someone's trying to intimidate me, and it's not going to work."

Before he could argue anymore, Tyler pulled up in the police cruiser.

This discussion wasn't over yet, though.

Madelyn mulled over their conversation as she sat in the back of the police cruiser. Zach sat in the front with Tyler, while Madelyn had some time alone to think. She pulled the blanket closer around her as the heat blared from the front. She still couldn't get warm, though. Her coolness started from inside her; it wasn't just the rain that left her chilled.

Zach Davis was trying to get her to leave town. When he'd asked those prodding questions about who would want her gone, his name was the only one that had risen to the surface.

Maybe Paula was right and he was an expert at manipulating people—including her. Maybe she'd been blinded by his good looks and his seemingly knight-in-shining-armor tactics.

She had to get a grip here, though.

Rain pounded on the windshield. The sky was still eerily dark, and thunder made the windshield vibrate. Tyler took his time traveling down the Lankford Highway. That was probably a good thing, since visibility was poor.

It only took thirty minutes to get back to Waterman's Reach. Instead of pulling up to her apartment, they stopped in front of a sprawling Victorian.

"This is Eva's bed-and-breakfast," Zach said. "She said you're more than welcome to stay here. I'd feel better with you here instead of by yourself."

But would he? Or was this just a part of his plan to appear like he was the good guy and throw her off his trail?

"Sounds good," she finally said, remembering that if she wanted answers, she needed to get on his good side.

"I'll stop by later with your clothes. I've got to figure out who sabotaged the boat earlier. I'll get Tyler to grab your suitcase. Does that work?"

"Sounds great." She reached into her pocket. "I suppose you still have the key?"

He nodded. "I haven't made it over to talk to Mayor Alan yet. I hope you don't think it's weird that I had the key last night?"

"No, of course not."

She hurried from the car before Zach could use his charm anymore and mess with her head. Before she even reached the front door, it opened and Eva stood there, warm smile in place.

"I'm so glad you're going to stay here. There's always safety in numbers, right?"

Madelyn smiled. "That's right."

Madelyn stepped inside the finely decorated home, already feeling like she should be more proper than she was. It was full of antiques and shiny wood and dainty collectibles, all done in a red, white and blue theme. The classic architecture was full of interesting angles and secluded nooks and intricate woodwork.

"Nice place," Madelyn said. "It has character."

"We like it. We opened it up a couple of years ago, but we haven't really gotten it off the ground yet." Eva took her arm and ushered her into the kitchen.

Before Madelyn could object, Eva gave her a polite nudge into the wooden chair by a bistro table. It became apparent that Madelyn wasn't going to get away with escaping to her room for a shower. Not yet, at least. "What did you do before you opened this and became the public relations liaison for the town?"

"What everyone else in town does—we were in the oyster business. I don't suppose we talked about this on that day we toured the town, did we?" Eva walked to the kitchen counter and grabbed a coffee mug.

Coffee…coffee sounded great.

"It must have paid pretty well." The statement slipped out before Madelyn could stop it. She immediately regretted her words. Her parents had raised her to be more polite than this. But a house like this required money. The decorating alone was probably a fortune and, unless the previous owners had restored this house, she could only imagine what kind of investment that was.

Madelyn knew this only because her parents had bought an old house in the country and restored it when she was in middle school. She'd seen the hard work and sweat they poured into the place. It had been their dream home.

Madelyn had been forced to sell it after they passed. She just couldn't keep up the expenses of the property.

"I don't know if I'd say that." Eva let out a nervous laugh and set the warm drink in front of Madelyn. "But we did well enough to start this. However, if business doesn't pick up here, we might have to look for another career choice. We're not quite close enough to retiring yet. Need some more money in the bank first."

Madelyn took a sip of the coffee and enjoyed the warmth that rushed through her. She felt exhausted: mentally, emotionally, even spiritually, if she was honest with herself.

Living without Jesus was living without hope.

She hadn't wanted to admit it, but it was true. She'd felt the change in her life over time as she'd moved further and further away from the foundation on which her parents had raised her. It was no wonder she felt so alone. She didn't even have the assurances of the Bible to bring her comfort anymore.

"Chief Davis is quite the lifesaver, isn't he?" Eva continued, lowering herself into the chair across from her.

Madelyn nodded, her bones beginning to ache again. It probably had something to do with her still-damp clothes. If she stayed in them much longer, she was sure to get sick.

She didn't want to be impolite, though, so she'd finish her coffee before excusing herself. "He's helped me on multiple occasions already, so I can't argue with that. It sounds like you like him?"

Eva nodded enthusiastically. "I personally think he's doing a fine job."

Her words made Madelyn pause. "But there are people who don't agree?"

She scoffed, as if she'd inadvertently brought up a sore subject. Madelyn suspected the woman knew exactly what she was doing. She seemed like the type who enjoyed to talk about town gossip.

"Levi—he's our former chief—thinks if Chief Davis does a good job it will ruin his reputation. It's hard sometimes with locals. They have trouble adjusting to newcomers."

"Aren't you a local?"

Eva shook her head. "I married into the town. Milton's family goes back three generations."

"Are you newlyweds?"

She laughed from deep in her belly. "Oh, no. We've been married more than thirty years. But to locals, I'll always be an outsider. I think some of the families around here take things overboard. We should always open our arms to new people in the community. If we don't, we're just going to die off. If we don't, this bed-and-breakfast has no hope of making it."

"Wise words."

"Anyway, I'll show you to your room. I've left a robe up there so you can change. I heard Tyler will be bringing your suitcase by shortly."

"Thank you," Madelyn said, truly grateful for the thoughtfulness of the people she'd met.

She hoped she didn't end up making any of them regret their kindness by putting them in the line of danger.

THIRTEEN

As the storm rolled off shore, Zach headed to the docks. He wanted to question the regulars there and see if anyone had seen someone messing with Ernie's boat. He knew that those who fished for their livelihood would be back on the water as soon as the danger passed. He bypassed going back to his place to change or get a cup of coffee. Time was of the essence right now.

There was no doubt in Zach's mind that the boat had been sabotaged.

Ernie and Rod were already back at the docks, telling everyone their tale like it was a feather in their cap. The two men stood by the fish-cleaning station, and a group of fishermen had gathered around them.

Zach cleared his throat, and the men stopped talking long enough to turn toward him. "Ernie, can I have a word?"

The old fisherman nodded and reluctantly left his audience. They stood a way from the crowd to talk. Zach was glad to see that Ernie seemed to be holding up well after all of the excitement from earlier. The man had a fresh mug of coffee in his hands and clean clothes on.

"I need to get an official statement from you," Zach started. "Can you walk through what happened on the boat again?"

Ernie nodded his head, sitting on a crude wooden bench overlooking the water. "It was the craziest thing. We were cruising along the water, enjoying the day, when all of the sudden the engine died. When I checked on it, a crack appeared in the hull of the boat right near the engine. Then, of all things, my radio wouldn't work. Makes no sense. No sense at all."

"I'm assuming you checked out the boat before you left?"

Ernie looked halfway offended as his eyes narrowed and his lips parted. "Just like I always do. This is my livelihood. I'm too old to keep fishing, so I've got to do something to make ends meet. I take my business seriously, Chief."

"I know you do. I just have to ask these questions. I'm trying to get to the bottom of what happened."

"Someone tampered with my boat. That's what happened."

Zach shifted, his notepad in hand. "Any idea who?"

Ernie rubbed his chin and sighed. "Not a one. I do my best to live at peace with people. No idea why someone might want to hurt me. Didn't do anything to anyone else."

"Anyone been messing with your boat lately? Have you let anyone borrow it?"

"No. That boat is my baby. No one else touches her."

"I'll write up a report—you'll need it to file a claim with your insurance company. I sent the marine police out to pick up the boat. We're going to send it to a mechanic to be evaluated."

"I appreciate it. Without my boat, I'm out of a job."

"I understand."

After Ernie walked away, Zach continued to question people who were regulars down at the docks. No one had seen anything. Ernie's boat was docked at the marina all the time. The area was generally locked up with a chain over the gate, but anyone who rented slip space here would have a key. Rod was getting Zach a list of everyone who had one.

As Zach headed back to his car, someone called his name. Zach looked up and saw a teen lingering behind Thad's Seafood. The boy waved at Zach, urging him to come closer.

"Can I help you?" Zach asked.

"I know I shouldn't say this," the boy started. His eyes darted around wildly, as if he feared someone might see him.

Zach recognized the boy as Rusty Peterson. He loved being on the water and took odd jobs with various fishermen and boat captains down at the docks when he wasn't in school.

Right now Rusty appeared stiff and his voice sounded higher pitched than normal. He was nervous, Zach realized. Really nervous.

"Say what, Rusty?"

Rusty looked around again. "I was out here early this morning. I wasn't supposed to be here, but I jumped the fence. I wanted a head start on the day. Now that the summer crowd is gone, I haven't been able to find as many jobs."

"What are you trying to tell me, Rusty?"

The teen frowned. "It's like this. I saw someone near Captain Ernie's boat when I got here. I'm not saying this person was tampering with it. But he was definitely lingering."

Zach's curiosity spiked. "Did this person get on the boat?"

Rusty shrugged. "I don't know. It didn't look like it. The person…he isn't a captain. He has his own boat slip at his house, and something told me he wasn't supposed to be there. But I knew that if I valued my job down here at the docks that I needed to stay quiet."

Zach glanced around, making sure no one was around to see this conversation. Everyone seemed distracted by Ernie and Rod, who continued to milk their story for all it was worth.

"Who was this person, Rusty?"

Rusty remained quiet. He rubbed his neck and glanced around. His breath had become shallower and a thin coat of sweat covered his forehead.

"Rusty, I'll use discretion," Zach told him.

Rusty's gaze came back to Zach, and he slowly nodded. He still looked uncertain, though. "Okay…it was Levi Watson."

Zach's eyebrows shot up. Had he heard correctly? He had to be sure. "The former police chief?"

Rusty nodded. "That's right. The one and only."

"Did Levi see you?"

Rusty shook his head. "I don't think so."

Since Zach had come to town, he'd suspected that Levi might have had something to do with the drug ring. Whoever was behind bringing those drugs into the country had somehow run the operation through this town. With Levi's connections and law enforcement background, he was a logical choice. If he wasn't in charge, he may have at least turned a blind eye to the operations. Zach needed proof, and he needed more names. That's why whenever he had time, he came to the docks and got to know the local fishermen.

Most of them seemed like honest, genuine people. They were a bit closed off and to themselves—leery of outsiders. But he didn't sense nefarious intentions.

The former chief was a different story. He'd only held animosity toward Zach since he'd arrived in town.

Was it because Zach had been hired over Watson's nephew Tyler? Possibly.

But what if those feelings ran deeper?

Zach couldn't pinpoint why Levi might want to run

Madelyn out of town. But he had to track down this lead and see where it took him.

"Thank you for your help, Rusty. I'll keep this between the two of us."

As he walked away, Zach decided to give Levi a visit. He wouldn't be greeted with open arms, nor would he be earning any likability points with the man. But Zach had a job to do, and he couldn't let someone's prominence in town deter him.

Ten minutes later, Zach stopped in front of the man's stately house. It was located on the water and far exceeded the amount Zach imagined the man had made as chief—at least based on his own salary now. Had this been a family home? Otherwise, how had Chief Watson afforded it?

But whoever had been importing those drugs had made a bundle of money. Houses and cars were usually the first place people spent some of their "hard earned" cash. He'd seen that enough from his days in Baltimore.

Levi answered on the first ring.

"Chief Davis," he said. "To what do I owe this honor?"

He could hear the sarcasm in his voice but ignored it. "I have a couple of questions I was hoping to ask you."

"Of course. Come in."

He stepped into the man's home, but Levi didn't offer to let him in any farther than the entrance. That was just as well with Zach.

"Levi, I need to ask you about something that happened down at the docks today," Zach started.

"What about it?"

"Captain Ernie's boat appears to have been tampered with. Someone placed you down at the docks this morning near the boat."

"That's ridiculous." He scoffed. "I was down at the marina this morning, but only because I left my fishing rod on Ernie's boat. We went out fishing together yesterday. Ask him."

"So you didn't mess with his radio or his engine?" Zach clarified.

Levi's face wrinkled. "Why would I?"

"That's what I'm trying to figure out."

The wrinkles disappeared and were replaced with color. Levi was getting angry, Zach realized.

"You need to be careful before you come in here accusing me of things," Levi said.

Zach shook his head. "I'm not accusing. I'm asking questions. You're the only person who's been placed near Ernie's boat."

"I've said all I'm going to say. I'll let you see yourself out. And don't come here accusing me again unless you have some evidence. Do you hear me? I'll run you out of town faster than a toupee in a nor'easter."

Zach heard him loud and clear, but he wasn't afraid of Levi's threats. He'd faced worse before.

Besides, if Levi wasn't hiding something, why did he react so strangely?

Zach stored the thought away for a later date, for a time when more evidence became clear.

By the time Madelyn was out of the shower, her suitcase had arrived. She'd normally dress to impress, but considering everything that had happened today, she had a feeling she'd be staying in for the rest of the day. For that reason, she pulled on her favorite yoga pants and a sweatshirt and then sat in the soft chair in the corner of her room. Right now, she simply needed to think.

The question at the forefront of her mind was: if not Zach, then who else might be behind these incidents? Who else could be responsible?

Her mind drew a blank. No one else here should have a

reason to want to run her out of town. Even if there were people who weren't crazy about bulking up tourism in the town, would they go to such desperate measures? She had a hard time believing the motive fit the means.

So how was all of this connected? Was she simply grasping at straws? Trying to see something that wasn't really there?

And what if—and it was a big what-if—Zach was just as much a victim in all of this as she was?

The leader in the Baltimore drug smuggling ring had never been caught. But if Zach was the guilty party here, why hadn't he taken the money and run? Why stay in law enforcement?

Which brought Madelyn to another question: What if Paula was wrong? What if Zach was simply trying to move on? To resume life after he'd lost everything?

If that was true, where did that leave Madelyn now? Who could be so desperate to hurt her? She had so many questions and so much that didn't make sense.

All she could do right now was to follow the evidence. If Zach was innocent, then there would be no proof of his involvement. If he was guilty, then the families of the victims of that shooting deserved to have justice. Her best choice was to put aside her emotions and let the facts speak for themselves.

Finally, she stood and stretched her back. As she glanced out the window, she saw Zach pull up. Interesting. What was he doing here? Her heart raced when she saw him, and she chided herself. She had to take control of her emotions and put an end to these feelings of attraction she felt toward the man.

Quietly, she crept downstairs, expecting Zach to have an update. To her surprise, he didn't come to the front door. She wandered around the house a moment before stopping near the screened-in porch at the back of the structure. One of the windows was open and voices drifted in.

Zach was talking to someone…but whom?

She knew she shouldn't, but she slipped behind a column and listened.

Zach appeared to be talking to Eva's husband. What was his name? Milton?

He still worked part-time in the aquaculture business. That's what Eva had told her in an earlier conversation when she'd fixed Madelyn some soup and watched as she ate every bite. She'd seen Eva and Milton's picture atop the piano in the hallway. The man was short with pale hair and skin that seemed out of place in this fishing community. It was clearly him talking to Zach.

"Listen, I appreciate you staying quiet about this," Zach said.

Something about the way he said the words caused Madelyn's suspicions to rise. Though her conscience cried out for her to stop, she pulled out her phone and opened her camera app. Everything in her wanted to turn a blind eye, to not do this. Zach had been kind to her. And he might be innocent. But if he wasn't, then this may be the evidence she needed to prove he was doing something illegal.

Her compassion was perhaps greater than her need for a good story. But she needed to end that. There was only one way to make sure that happened. She had to put her emotions—as wishy-washy as they were—aside. She'd collect her facts and then decide what the truth was, based on the evidence she gathered.

Her logic didn't change the sick feeling that gurgled in her gut, though.

Her dread deepened even more when she saw Zach pull something out of his pocket.

It was a package. As he handed it to Milton, Madelyn snapped a picture. Was this just the evidence she'd been searching for? She stared at the photo on her screen. He certainly looked suspicious in the image. The way his shoulders hunched. How his head was lowered. The secret way he handed Milton the package.

Quickly, she turned her phone off and hurried back upstairs. Now she had to decide what exactly she would do with this.

Because as much as she tried to be tough, she was still having trouble believing the chief was a bad person.

FOURTEEN

With a touch of hesitation, Zach knocked on Madelyn's door. He told himself he needed to talk to her about the case. But the truth was that he wanted to see her. Only in a professional sense, he told himself. After all, he needed to check on her after everything that had happened. It had nothing to do with the fact that he was attracted to her.

Zach had confirmed with Ernie that he and Levi had gone out fishing yesterday. So Levi did have an alibi in that sense. But the man still could have tampered with the boat. On top of that, Ernie had mentioned to Levi that he was doing a tour with Madelyn today.

What Zach couldn't figure out was why. Why would Levi want to harm Madelyn? It didn't make any sense.

Footsteps padded against the floor on the other side of the door. Madelyn cracked the door a second later, a whoosh of lilac rushing out and making his heart speed up. He'd already come to associate that scent with Madelyn.

The breath left his lungs at the mere glimpse of her. She looked different. Gone were the fancy clothes and perfect makeup and flawless hair. He'd seen her absent of those things on the boat when she'd been rescued. But this was different. Her still-damp hair had a touch of wave to it. Her cheeks were rosy. Her clothing—yoga pants and a

T-shirt—was casual, but at the same time seemed flat-tering.

She looked simpler. More natural.

And he liked it.

But the look in Madelyn's eyes was close to tortured. What was going on in that head of hers? How much more could happen to her before she broke?

She didn't offer to open the door any more than a crack. Maybe she was being modest or maybe Zach had caught her in the middle of something. Maybe she was simply cautious after everything that happened.

"Hey," she said softly.

"Can we talk a moment, Madelyn?"

She rubbed her lips together before nodding. "Sure thing. Can I meet you downstairs?"

"Of course."

A few minutes later, she joined him in the screened-in porch at the back of the house. Her gaze skittered around the space in a way that made him curious. What exactly was she looking for? She almost appeared to be expecting someone to jump out and grab her.

"There's no one here," he murmured. Eva and Milton had run to the grocery store, so Zach and Madelyn would have some privacy for a moment. He'd just spoken with Milton himself about another matter and to give him a heads-up on the situation with Madelyn. If someone wanted to harm her, Zach hoped they wouldn't go through Eva and Milton to do so. But both needed to be on guard.

Madelyn nodded and shoved a hair behind her ear. "Good to know."

She sat in a white wicker chair across from him. An after-the-rain breeze fluttered through the air, bringing with it the scent of the passing storm: grass, leaves and dampness. She'd put a sweatshirt on and pulled it closer around her.

Zach sat in the chair beside her, a glass-top table with a cheerful sunflower in a bottle between them. He needed to broach this conversation carefully. If he said too much, it would only lead to trouble.

"Madelyn, I wanted to find out if there was anything else you could remember about what happened today," he started. "Was there anything unusual about the boat? Anything that caused alarm before all the problems started?"

She narrowed her eyes and pushed some hair behind her ear. As she let out a soft sigh, she pulled her knees up to her chest. "I don't think so. I mean, I don't know much about boats."

She almost looked like she was trying to protect herself. Zach had learned to read body language a long time ago. When people crossed their arms or put objects between themselves and another person, usually it was because some kind of internal guard was going up.

Her body language reminded him that she was hiding something. Would she ever trust him enough to tell him what? He'd put his life on the line for her, yet she remained tight-lipped. Why?

She stared out one of the screened panels. He followed her gaze and saw a neighbor's beagle exploring a corner of the backyard now that the storm had passed.

"Madelyn, before you came here, did you have connections with Levi Watson?"

Her gaze swerved toward his. "Levi Watson?"

"The former police chief."

Her eyes widened as realization washed over her. "You think he's behind this?"

Zach raised his hand to cease that thought. "I'm not saying that at all. I just want to know if you've ever had any interaction with him?"

She shrugged. "I met him that first day I was in town,

when Eva gave me a tour. We ran into him at the café. That was it."

"What was your conversation like?"

"It was unremarkable. He said it was nice to meet me, he was glad I was here and if this article managed to bring tourists in town, he'd be shocked."

Zach raised his eyebrows. "He said that last part?"

Madelyn nodded. "That's right. I thought it was weird, but Eva said that Levi is one of the people who doesn't want the town to grow. He likes Waterman's Reach like it is now."

So maybe the former chief was trying to run Madelyn out of town to prevent her from writing the article? Would he really take things this far, though?

"A lot of people resist change," Madelyn said, almost as if she could read his thoughts.

"It gives him motive."

She frowned. "You really think he could be behind this?"

"I'm not implying anything," Zach said, rising to his feet. "I'm just trying to find one decent lead."

She jumped to her feet, as well. "Where are you going?"

"Honestly? I'm going back to my house to finally get cleaned up after everything that's happened today. I'm bringing some files there so I can review them."

"Can I come with you?" she said.

He raised his eyebrows. "To my house?"

Her cheeks flushed. "Let me review the evidence with you. Maybe something will spark a memory or connection. Besides, I'd feel better doing something and not being alone."

"What about your article?"

"I'll bring my notes with me and work on it there." She paused, her eyes imploring him. "I promise I won't get in your way."

Hesitantly, he nodded. "Okay. Maybe a second set of eyes will be helpful."

He hoped he didn't regret this.

Madelyn hoped she didn't regret this.

Something had clicked in her mind when she was talking to Zach at the B and B. She realized she had to find some answers. She had to take risks. And the more time she spent with Zach, the more likely it was she could discover new information about him.

She'd spontaneously decided to ask to come here. She did want to look over the case files. But she also wanted to snoop.

"Help yourself to anything in the fridge," Zach said as they walked into his living room. "There's not much. And keep the doors locked."

Madelyn nodded. "Got it."

"I need to take a warm shower and get some clean clothes on. The files are on the table by my desk. You can look through them. There shouldn't be anything there that you don't already know, but feel free to take a gander. Maybe a fresh set of eyes will help."

"You never know."

As Zach stepped toward the bathroom, Madelyn went to his desk and sat down. When she heard the door click shut, she stared at his computer.

Madelyn knew she shouldn't do it. But how could she not? This might be her only chance to look through Zach's things. In fact, the opportunity had practically been handed to her. She could potentially find the answers she needed.

She glanced at her phone. The picture of Zach exchanging something with Milton stared back at her. What was that about?

She didn't have time to dwell on it now.

Moving quickly, she turned on the computer screen. As it booted up, her gaze went to the drawers of the hefty desk. With a touch of guilt, she opened the first one. Pencils, pens and paper clips stared back her.

She opened the next one. Bills. She flipped through a few of them, but they all seemed like the normal power, cell-phone and car-insurance notifications.

The bottom drawer held envelopes and paper.

She frowned. She wasn't getting very far here.

Water from the shower still roared through the pipes. But she had to move quickly. She rushed to the other side of the desk. In the bottom drawer, there were some file folders. Her heart raced. Maybe there was something here. Maybe.

She picked up the first one. The tab read Baltimore. Inside, there were dozens of articles on the shooting there. Most witnesses had pointed to Zach as being the bad guy. In fact, she'd read several of these write-ups already while doing her research.

The next folder was the police report. It looked like it had been photocopied. Was Zach allowed to do that? She wasn't sure.

Looking at the information, it appeared Zach had written all of these. These must have been the reports about the gang, leading up to the confrontations where lives had been lost. She quickly scanned the information there. Most of it she knew.

Some potent heroin had been brought into the city. Three people had already been arrested and found to be using this particular kind of heroin. Those three people were also guilty of violent crimes: a murder, a rape and an attempted homicide.

It appeared this certain kind of heroin was especially deadly and made people act irrationally. Despite that, people were still using it. Zach had been trying to pinpoint its origin.

He'd thought he'd discovered the gang responsible for distributing the drug. He'd set up a bust. But things had turned ugly quickly. Two officers were shot. Zach had no choice but to pull the trigger and take down one of the gang members.

Someone had to take the blame for the fallen officers. Zach seemed to be the scapegoat.

That's not what Paula thought. She thought he'd acted irresponsibly. That he was macho and arrogant. That he'd been involved and was trying not to get caught.

That wasn't the person Madelyn had been getting to know, though.

The final folder stared at her on the bottom of the drawer. Her hands trembled slightly as she picked it up. Inside, there were letters.

She was supposed to be looking for a pattern here of arrogance and shady decisions. Was this her evidence?

Part of her didn't want to read it.

She did anyway.

I thought I could trust you. I thought you were different. But you're a bottom-line guy too, aren't you? That's really all that matters at the end of the day, isn't it? You're not different than any of the rest of them.

Her eyes traveled to the bottom of the letter. It was signed "Mario Williams."

She sucked in a deep breath. He was the gang member who'd died.

Was this the proof she needed that Zach had inside connections with the drug ring?

Madelyn's stomach constricted.

Was this part of the evidence she needed for her article? Would this help to prove once and for all that Zach deserved to serve prison time for his negligence in the undercover sting?

Instead of making her feel relieved, her gut dropped with dread.

A door clicked in the distance. Madelyn quickly shoved the papers back into the drawer and slammed it shut. Sweat sprinkled across her forehead. She was supposed to be reviewing the case. Where was that folder?

She nervously stared at the desk, hoping that Zach didn't realize her true intentions for wanting to be in his house... or in this town.

FIFTEEN

Quickly, Madelyn found the folder on the table behind her and grabbed it. She opened it, trying desperately to look like she'd been studying it the whole time.

Zach's footsteps sounded across the wood floor, each step causing Madelyn's nerves to tighten. Would he sense she was deceiving him?

"Anything stand out to you?" Zach asked.

Her throat tightened as she shook her head. "Unfortunately, no."

Madelyn waited for his response, halfway expecting him to call her bluff. He strode over and peered at the file in her hands.

"That's what I figured. But it was worth a try, right?"

She released her breath. Zach wasn't on to her. Thank goodness. "Right."

As he leaned in close to study the reports, Madelyn was keenly aware of his presence. Her heart raced. She took a deep breath of his woodsy cologne, the scent alluring and one she could get used to.

"The answers are here somewhere." He jabbed his finger into the file. "We just have to find them."

Just then his phone rang. He glanced at the screen. "It's Mayor Alan. I've got to take this."

"Of course."

As Zach disappeared into a room down the hallway, she turned back to the case files and tried to concentrate on the facts there. But her hands trembled. Maybe she wasn't cut out for this kind of thing. No amount of prodding, encouragement or pushing would change that.

That letter from Mario just might be the proof she needed of wrongdoing on Zach's part. Did it solidify the fact that Zach was somehow involved in all of this? Her gut told her no. But how else could she explain it?

Just then her phone buzzed. She recognized Paula's number. It was almost like her boss could sense Madelyn's inner turmoil and had timed her call perfectly.

With a touch of hesitation, Madelyn answered. "Hey."

"What's going on? Any updates for me?"

She thought about everything that had happened and considered what to tell her. Not what she'd seen today. She wasn't ready to share that yet. But she had to tell Paula something. Paula was her boss. Madelyn was here on work time, not just for leisure or to do what she wanted.

"I got a picture," she finally said.

"A picture? What kind of picture?"

Madelyn frowned, feeling like she was betraying Zach. But she was sent here to do a job. She had to push her emotions aside.

She lowered her voice, fearful that Zach might hear her. "Zach was handing over an envelope with someone. It all looked hush-hush."

"That's interesting. Send it to me."

"I'm not sure there's anything you can do with it. I don't think it means anything." Guilt gnawed at her. Madelyn regretted the revelation as soon as it'd left her lips.

"There it is again," Paula said, that scolding tone to her voice.

"There's what?"

"You're getting soft on me."

"No, I'm not." But even as Madelyn said the words, she knew they weren't true. Her compassion could be her best or worst attribute. Even her parents had said that. They'd been afraid that one day her empathy would get her in trouble and had tried to guide her to use wisdom in her emotions.

"Arrogant police officers need to be punished," Paula said. "Officers like the one who killed your parents. It was wrong that he got away with it. We can't let that happen again."

Madelyn glanced at the door where Zach had disappeared. "I'm just not convinced that he's guilty."

"Don't listen to your emotions. Listen to me. Remember your parents. Do this for them."

Paula's words somehow hit home. Her *parents*. If she focused on getting justice for them, maybe she would be able to pull through this.

"I'll send you the picture," she finally said, still uncertain if this was the right thing or not. If she proved beyond a doubt that Zach was innocent, then no one else ever had to see that photo. She'd delete it and it would be of no use. She had to keep that in mind.

"Good girl. Keep getting to know him. You're on the right track. He'll open up to you in no time."

Madelyn hung up and then found the photo on her phone. She nibbled on her lips before sending the picture. She hoped she didn't regret this.

As soon as she hit Send, her gut twisted.

Had Madelyn just made the biggest mistake of her life? Or had she just secured a successful career for her future?

Zach was surprised when he walked back into his kitchen fifteen minutes later and smelled the pleasant aroma of food. What was that? Garlic. He heard something sizzling.

It had been a long time since his house smelled like this. He normally grabbed a sandwich or a can of soup. Home-cooked meals were a thing of the past. His stomach instantly rumbled.

Some food sounded good, especially after his conversation with the mayor. He frowned and set aside those thoughts for a moment. He'd deal with his problems with the mayor later.

He stepped into the kitchen and saw Madelyn standing over the stove managing three pots and pans. She smiled when she spotted him.

"You said help myself to anything I could find in the fridge," she said. "So I did. I figured you needed to eat. I haven't seen you do much of that since all of the mayhem started."

"I could use a bite to eat. I just didn't know there was this much food in my house."

"I found some ground beef, canned green beans and a few potatoes. This is nothing fancy, but I threw together some Salisbury steaks, mashed potatoes and a vegetable. My mom always said that last one in particular was important."

Zach could hardly pull his eyes away. There was something about the scene that made a new emotion grow in his gut. Before, he'd been attracted to Madelyn. But seeing her in his home, looking like she belonged...that made visions of something long-term pop into his head.

He reminded himself that Madelyn was leaving soon. And that he didn't want to date. That he had other things to concentrate on.

But it couldn't hurt to sit down for a meal. To talk. To connect with someone else.

It had been a long time since he'd allowed himself to trust. It had been a long time since he'd *wanted* to trust.

But he felt that changing at the moment.

Madelyn glanced behind her before flipping a Salisbury steak on the stove. "Why don't you have a seat? Everything is almost ready."

"I'll grab some drinks," he said.

"Sounds good." She began plating up the food. She smiled almost sheepishly as she brought the plates to the table. "It's nothing fancy. Have I said that yet?"

"It's better than bachelor food." He set the glasses on the table and sat down. "Most nights, it's microwave dinners or mac and cheese."

She shrugged. "I understand. I don't cook much for myself. Cooking for one isn't much fun."

"I can understand that." He shifted as she sat down. "Look, do you mind if I pray for the food before we eat?"

An unknown emotion washed across her face. "Not at all."

He lifted up a prayer of thanks and a plea for safety and guidance in all that was happening before saying amen.

Madelyn took her first bite and then wiped her mouth. "My mom was an excellent cook. She always said food was a great cure for the ails of life. She seemed to have a recipe for anything. Chicken soup for colds, cupcakes for sad days, bacon for…well, almost anything."

He smiled. "I think I would have liked your mom."

A cloud seemed to cover her face as she sat down. "I think you would have also."

"I know you said they were in a car accident. Do you mind if I ask what happened?" His appetite, once hearty, was now waning. He wasn't sure he wanted to ask the question, but another part of him sensed Madelyn needed to talk.

Her face looked pinched, and she seemed to have lost her appetite also. She merely played with her food. "A police officer pursuing a suspect ran into them when they were on their way home from dinner. They died instantly. I was supposed to be with them that night, but I wasn't feeling well, so I stayed with a friend instead."

"Wow. I'm so sorry." His voice caught.

She nodded stiffly, obviously trying to keep her emotions at bay. She gave up eating and put her fork down. "My life hasn't been the same since then."

"No one's would be." His own parents were both alive and well, enjoying their retirement with cruises in Alaska and visits to Caribbean resorts.

"The officer was pursuing a robbery suspect. My parents apparently didn't see them coming. The perpetrator got away, but my parents' lives ended."

What she said washed over him. "The officer hit them?"

She nodded slowly, stoically. "Somehow he walked away unscathed."

"That's got to be hard to stomach. I can't even imagine. Did the officer lose his job?"

She pressed her lips together and averted her gaze, obviously struggling. "He was on desk duty for a while. Last I heard, he'd been promoted. Time not only heals all wounds, it erases all wrongdoings, I suppose."

A sick feeling gurgled in his stomach. He wanted to reach out, to grab her hand. But he didn't. He couldn't. The timing wasn't right. If he allowed himself to become vulnerable, he might lose his focus.

"Sometimes police officers have to make split-second decisions. Sometimes they don't do this very wisely, and people get hurt." His voice became hoarser as he said the words.

Her gaze fluttered to meet his, and questions lingered there. "You sound like you know something about that."

Zach licked his lips, wondering how much he should say. He hadn't spoken with anyone here about what had happened. He imagined how freeing it would feel to open up to someone. And why not the pretty travel reporter who was having dinner with him?

For a moment, he set aside his doubts about Madelyn, his idea that she was hiding something. He would talk— only talk. No touching. No gravitating toward her. No entertaining ideas of more than the relationship they had right now. He could handle that.

"Back when I was a detective in Baltimore, I was involved in an undercover drug sting that went wrong. I lost two of my guys, and one of the gang members died, as well."

"I'm sorry. Is that why you came here? For a fresh start?"

"I resigned." He nodded slowly, mournfully. "Of course, that was never really reported. I was in charge, so I took responsibility for the outcome. There are three families whose lives have been changed forever, and I'll live with that every day for the rest of my life."

"Three families?"

"My officers and the drug dealer."

"You even mourn for the bad guys, huh?"

He shrugged, considering his words before answering. "I don't take any of the decisions I make lightly. I can't. Not when people's lives and futures are on the line."

"Do you miss the life of being a big-city detective?"

"I think everything happens for a purpose. I lost everything after that, Madelyn." Why was he opening up to her like this? Probably because it felt good to come clean. He'd stayed quiet about this since he'd come to town. So why did he think he could trust her? "My job was gone, my reputation, my fiancée even left me. But that was nothing compared to what those families lost."

Her gaze appeared stormy and troubled. "I guess that drug bust was pretty important?"

Two years of his life had hinged upon investigating the drug trafficking. It all culminated at that bust. Things hadn't ended the way he wanted. "This drug was messing up people. Crime was up in the city because of it. I had to find the source before even more people got hurt."

"Did you?"

"No. Some of the key players got away before we could. Any information my informants had collected was also lost. All of the months they spent embedding themselves with the gang was for nothing."

"I'm sorry," she whispered.

Her words had a lot of depth and were tinged with an unknown emotion. Was there something she wasn't saying? Because her apology kept echoing in his head in a way that made him wonder.

SIXTEEN

Madelyn's heart leaped into her throat as she stared across the table at Zach. She couldn't go through with this article. She couldn't.

She'd been wrong. Paula had been wrong.

Zach was nothing like the cold-blooded killer who'd taken the lives of her parents.

What was Madelyn going to do? How could she make this right?

They finished their dinner, and she collected the plates. This had begun to feel a little too intimate, too personal. It was easier when Zach was just a name, just a news story. But that was no longer the case. He'd become a person—a person that Madelyn was beginning to care about.

She filled the sink with soapy water to do dishes, desperate to do something to keep her thoughts occupied.

"I can get that."

His deep voice made her shiver. "I don't mind."

"Then let me help you." He rolled up his sleeves and grabbed a dish towel.

Heat traveled from her heart all the way up to her cheeks. She had fond memories of her mom and dad doing this exact thing. They'd been such a team in every way. She longed for those simple days again, days when she felt secure and loved and like part of a unit.

Why was there a seed of hope in her that maybe she could have that with Zach?

She had to get focused here. She pointed at the Scripture hung near the window by the sink. "'Trust in the Lord with all your heart.' You believe that's the way to live?"

"Sometimes trust in the Lord is all you're left with." He grabbed the plate she'd just washed and began to towel dry it.

"Sometimes trusting in God only lets you down." Her words sounded raw and honest, but she refused to take them back.

"I'm sorry you feel that way. I know you've been through a lot, and it may seem like God abandoned you."

"I guess I've been leaning a lot on my own understanding. It seems impossible not to."

"That's where faith comes in." He dried another plate.

"I wish it were that easy for me." She washed the last dish and handed it to him, ready to be finished with this conversation—wishing she'd never started it for that matter. She already felt exposed, as if she'd shown parts of her heart to Zach that she'd kept closed for years. She sensed Zach was feeling the same way.

Her facade wasn't going to hold up for much longer. If she wasn't careful, she'd end up pouring out everything to the very man she was supposed to be investigating. She couldn't let that happen.

"I should probably go. It's getting late." She placed the dish towel back on the sink.

Zach nodded. "I'll drive you."

His hand went to her lower back as he led her outside to his car. His touch seemed to burn through her clothing and into her skin.

She was in trouble. A lot of trouble.

When he'd tucked her securely in the passenger seat, he ran around into the driver's side. They were silent as they cruised down the road toward the bed-and-breakfast. There didn't seem to be any words to follow up their previous conversation. They didn't have enough time to delve into any deep topics.

Finally, they pulled up to the bed-and-breakfast. Madelyn was ready to simply say thanks and hop out of the car. Before she could, Zach was already out and opening her door. He walked her to the porch.

She hated to admit it, but, despite everything that had happened, the night seemed perfect. The wind was sweet and gentle. The crickets chanted. An owl hooted from somewhere not far away.

They faced each other on the porch, but as Madelyn tried to say something, her voice caught in her throat. Zach stood in front of her, his eyes warm and kind. It seemed natural for her to lay her hand on his chest.

Just a friendly gesture to say good-night.

But she knew that wasn't true.

Zach stepped closer. His eyes were smoky, cloaked with emotion.

"Madelyn," he started.

Her throat tightened with anticipation. "Yes?"

Before he could finish his statement or lean any closer, a loud bang sounded in the background. Zach pushed Madelyn behind him as he turned toward the sound.

A car backfiring. That was all. Madelyn nearly wanted to laugh. Everything that had happened lately had conditioned her to think the worst.

As Zach turned back to her, she realized how close they were standing. Close enough to kiss. Close enough that she craved his touch.

She'd fallen for Zach, she realized. Despite everything, she was beginning to fall in love with the man.

"Madelyn—" he started, leaning closer.

Just as he reached for her, the porch light came on and Eva appeared at the door.

Zach and Madelyn quickly stepped back from each other, the moment broken.

"I heard something and wanted to check that everything was okay," Eva rushed.

"It was just a car backfiring," Zach explained.

The older woman put a hand over her heart before letting out a nervous laugh. "I'm so glad. After those gunshots the other day, I've been on guard. So has most of the town. I hope you'll be able to track down the person responsible."

"I'm doing my best, Eva."

Madelyn glanced at Zach, knowing the moment couldn't be regained. Not tonight, at least. And maybe that was for the best. Even though her heart seemed to long for something more.

Zach inched closer toward the steps leading off the porch. "I'll talk to you later," he told Madelyn.

She pulled her arms across her chest and offered a small smile. "Sounds good."

With that, he walked back to his cruiser.

Madelyn's heart was still racing from her almost kiss with Zach. Was she crazy? Thank goodness Eva had stopped them in time. She already had enough trouble without adding guy problems to the list.

After chitchatting with Eva for a few minutes, Madelyn escaped back to her room. She had to call Paula and put an end to all of this.

"Tell me about the picture," was the first thing Paula said. No *Hello*. No *How are you*. Only *Tell me about the picture*.

Guilt pounded at Madelyn. "I don't know what was going on, Paula. I just saw the exchange happening and thought it looked a little suspicious. That's when I snapped the picture."

"You know who that man is, right?"

"Milton Rogers. I'm staying at his house. It's a bed-and-breakfast."

"Madelyn, I think Zach is in cahoots with the very people who brought the drugs up here to Maryland."

Madelyn dropped into a chair and leaned back, emotionally and physically exhausted from everything that had happened since she'd been in town. "You've mentioned that before."

"I heard rumor that the heroin that was the focus of Zach's investigation came from somewhere down there near the mouth of the Chesapeake Bay. I bet that's why Zach is in Waterman's Reach. I think he was working with these drug dealers. I think he shot Mario Williams in order to keep him quiet about his role in all of this."

Madelyn remembered that letter she'd found. Should she share what she'd read? Pressure built between her shoulders. She couldn't bring herself to do it. Not yet, at least.

"That doesn't make sense, Paula." She just didn't think that Zach had it in him to be that deceptive.

"You're being blinded by your compassion again. Think about it, Madelyn. Milton is from down in that area. I know he lives in a large house and drives a nice car. How do you think he got that money?"

"You think he got it through drugs?"

"Not only that, but I think he paid Zach off. That's why Zach is down there now, because he's turning a blind eye to the drugs as they come and go in the bay."

Madelyn nibbled on her lip, conflicting emotions clashing inside. Where did her loyalties lie? Was it with Paula and her career with the magazine? Was it with Zach, someone she just met a few days ago, but who had saved her life on more than one occasion? No, she decided her loyalty was with the truth. She just had to uncover what that was.

"I've gotten to know Zach," she finally said, reserving her judgment. "I can't see him doing that."

"You're being persuaded by his good looks. You can't trust him, Madelyn. I thought you were the right person for this job. Was I wrong?"

Madelyn wanted to just give all of this up. It felt like more than she could handle—more than she wanted to handle.

"How do you know all of this about Milton?" Madelyn had included the man's name when she sent the picture earlier.

"I did my research—like any good reporter would."

Feelings of inadequacy flooded her. Had Madelyn fallen behind on the job? Was she letting her own emotions cloud her judgment?

"Madelyn, when all of this is over, Zach is going to be in prison. Whatever you think you may be feeling for him now isn't worth the heartache that's to come. You're going to go back to being alone. You'll have lost your chance to make something for yourself as a reporter, and you're going to throw that away for a good-looking guy? There are a lot of men out there who will make your heart race. Don't give everything up for this guy."

Her words felt like a slap in the face. "I never said I was going to give everything up. I didn't even say that I had feelings for Zach."

"You didn't have to."

Madelyn bit down the frustration rising inside her. "But Paula, have you considered that you might be wrong?"

Silence strained between them. "I know this case better than anyone. I'm not wrong."

"If you know this case so well, why did you send me down here to do the article?" The question had been circling in her mind for a while now, but she hadn't wanted to ask it. She wanted to believe that Paula had sent her here because she felt Madelyn was the best woman for the job. On the other hand, Paula was a control freak. This seemed like a job she would have wanted to do herself.

"Because I'm the editor in chief. I don't have the time to do the legwork. I want to see you succeed. Don't you want that? Isn't that what's important in life? You can have financial security, a nice nest egg, a reliable car and desirable house to live in. We might as well enjoy our time on this earth while we've got it."

"I see." That thought harshly contradicted Madelyn's thoughts of eternal life. At one time she'd believed that there was much more to live for than what this world had to offer. She missed that perspective that she used to have. Was it too late to get it back?

"Don't go soft on me, Madelyn."

Madelyn scowled. "I'm not."

"You've got a job to do. I expect results."

Madelyn pinched the skin between her eyes. "I understand."

"Don't disappoint me."

The words echoed in her head. But who did Madelyn fear disappointing more? Paula? Herself? Or how about God? Because whatever decision she made, she was the one who'd have to live with it for the rest of her life.

Zach bumped down the road the next morning, Madelyn beside him. He was going to one of the regional marinas this morning. The state police had taken Ernie's boat there to be inspected by one of their mechanics. Zach wanted to see for himself what had happened to the watercraft.

Since all of this crime had started happening in town over this past week, Zach couldn't stop wondering if there was any connection with what had happened in Baltimore. He had to get to the bottom of this before he lost everything— again. His job, his reputation and the people who trusted him.

All he'd had since then was his faith. His faith was enough; he knew that. But he wanted to make things right.

Madelyn sat beside him, a laptop on her lap as she worked on her story.

"How's it going?" he asked, glancing over at her. Her glossy brown hair gently fell in her face. She wore crisp, professional black pants with a striped blue top. He could stare at her all day. "Have you gotten everything you need for your article?"

She nodded. "Yes, I told Eva I didn't need any more tours today. She wanted to introduce me to some artists and let me see their studios. I guess there's a vineyard on the outskirts of town and another restaurant farther up the bay. I'll get there eventually. I want to use the information I have first."

Zach stole another glance at her. Despite his better instincts, he hadn't been able to stop thinking about her all night. Especially about their near kiss. Why was he letting her have this effect on him?

Madelyn was coming with him today purely for safety reasons. Until he knew more details about what was going on, he felt better knowing she was with him, that she was safe. It had nothing to do with his rapidly growing feelings for the woman.

Finally, they pulled up to the repair shop. After asking a couple of guys on the dock, they ambled toward the man who owned the place. Washington was his name, and he was an older man whose face was full of wrinkles, wrinkles that could probably tell hours worth of stories about life on the water. He was thin, wore overalls, but somehow still appeared spritely. The state police claimed he was the best in the area.

The man looked up from a clipboard as they approached. "Can I help you?"

Zach introduced himself and flashed his badge. "I'm

looking for information on a Tracker that was brought in here by the state police yesterday. I'm the police chief from Waterman's Reach."

Washington nodded and led them into a bay. Ernie's boat was there.

"Yep, I spent yesterday looking at this girl. Definitely tampered with. There were pry marks near the engine. Someone loosened it up just enough that it would cause a crack as the boat got moving faster."

Zach nodded, his thoughts churning. "How about the radio?"

"Two wires were cut. It was simple but effective. This situation could have turned out a lot worse. It's a good thing the people on board were able to get to dry land before that storm came."

Zach nodded. "I agree."

There were no other questions he could ask. Washington had simply confirmed what Zach already suspected: someone was out to harm Madelyn. The thought disturbed him.

As they started home, Zach glanced into his rearview mirror. He blinked at what he saw. Was that…the white truck?

He stared harder, straightening in his seat. It was. The truck was behind them again!

"You see it, too?" Madelyn asked, her gaze flickering to the side-view mirror.

"Unfortunately." Zach suddenly jerked the steering wheel, and they swerved into a U-turn. "It's time to end this. Hold on."

When his cruiser stopped, they faced the white truck head-on. The driver opposite them threw on the brakes.

Without hesitation, Zach charged toward him, lights and siren blaring. The truck turned and gunned it. Zach raced down the road. But the truck was just as fast and didn't let up.

It turned off the main road onto a side street. Zach stayed on its tail, determined to end this once and for all. There was still too much distance between the vehicles to easily catch up.

The rural road was narrow, surrounded mostly by farms. The landscape blurred around them as the chase continued.

"I can't let him get away this time," Zach muttered.

Ahead there was a small bridge crossing over the river. The structure looked low and old.

Madelyn gasped as they headed toward it.

Suddenly, the truck flew off the bridge. The vehicle seemed to remain suspended in the air a moment. Zach couldn't look away as he waited to see what would happen next.

The truck landed with a huge splash in the water. A moment later, a man wearing a baseball cap, sunglasses and an oversize leather coat scrambled from the vehicle. He trudged through the water toward a nearby pier across the river.

Zach raced to the opposite side of the river and threw his cruiser in Park. He rushed out. But it was too late. The man jumped on a waiting Jet Ski.

He'd obviously left the watercraft there, keys in the ignition. Because once he got on, he zoomed off.

Zach knew just as well as anyone that, without a boat, there was no catching this guy now.

They'd been close. So close.

SEVENTEEN

As Zach and Madelyn headed back to Waterman's Reach later that day, Zach's radio beeped. They'd been at the bridge for the past two hours, talking with state police and neighbors after the chase involving the white truck. The state police were running the license plate numbers, but, as of now, they still had no answers.

Madelyn hoped once the truck had been recovered from the water and dried out that it might offer some clues. But, until then, she just had to be patient.

"Chief, it's Rod at the marina," Madelyn heard Lynn say over the radio. "They've found something in the water he said you'd want to see immediately."

"Something I want to see?" Zach questioned.

"That's all he said, Chief."

"Can you send Tyler?"

"Tyler is tied up with a traffic accident on the highway. He said he's at least fifteen minutes out."

"I'll be right there." Zach glanced at Madelyn. "You may have to wait a minute on that ride home after all."

Madelyn didn't argue. Her curiosity was spiked. "I understand."

Zach flicked the lights on and raced through town toward the marina. As he traveled, his phone rang. He frowned when he looked at the screen.

"It's the mayor again."

Her thoughts traveled back to Zach's rather gray demeanor after his conversation with the mayor that day she'd snooped in his desk at his house. He'd tried to brush it off, but the conversation must have been more intense than she realized.

"One minute." Zach answered the phone, his Bluetooth broadcasting the conversation throughout the car. "I apologize in advance that you have to hear this."

"Chief Davis," the mayor started, his voice hard and without any trace of friendliness. "In case I haven't made this clear, I'm concerned about everything that's been happening in town."

Zach frowned, keeping his eyes on the road. "I have been also. I can assure you that I've been working on it nonstop."

"Good. I'm glad to hear that. But there's more. I understand some of these crimes that have occurred are linked directly to you. That's what the talk of the town is."

"Directly to me?" He remained calm despite the implications of the mayor's words. "What do you mean?"

"I heard there was blood in your kitchen. Gunshots fired at you. Now you're trying to place the blame on Levi Watson?"

Madelyn cast a sharp look at Zach. Small town politics were coming into play here, and if the mayor knew that Madelyn was listening to this conversation, she was sure he'd change his rhetoric. So much for making a good impression.

Zach continued to race toward town. "I'm following every lead. That's my job."

"There are a lot of people in town who don't trust outsiders. You're giving them reason not to. Levi Watson is a hero to most. People think you're deflecting attention from yourself by focusing on Watson."

Zach let out a soft sigh. "Mayor, with all due respect,

you've got to know that I wouldn't do these things. And if I did—and that's a big *if*—I wouldn't leave the evidence anywhere that's connected with me."

"If word of everything that's happened gets leaked, tourism will essentially shut down in this town before it even starts. You need to bring an end to this crime spree. Now. And stop throwing out accusations."

Was that what this whole conversation was about? Tourism? Madelyn knew it was important to Waterman's Reach, but she had no idea it was this important. No, she'd assumed the risk on people's lives would be greater.

Zach clenched his jaw. "I've brought the state police in to help. I'm using all of the resources available to me to figure out what's going on."

"Do you have any ideas? Any clue as to what this is all about?"

"I wish I could say I do. I've wondered if someone's trying to run me out of town."

"These measures seem a little extreme for that, don't they?" Mayor Alan asked.

"Perhaps. But I've seen people go to great lengths to get what they want."

Was Zach hinting about what had happened in Baltimore? Madelyn's pulse spiked.

"I expect you to keep me in the loop," the mayor continued.

"Of course. You'll have a full report by the end of the week." Zach hit End and then glanced at Madelyn. "Sorry you had to hear that."

"That was pretty intense," Madelyn said. The whole interaction seemed odd. It was too full of politics and assumptions and strong-arming. Though Madelyn had initially had a good impression of the mayor, that was starting to change. "I can't believe he's so closed-minded."

Zach frowned. "This is what happens in close-knit communities sometimes. No one can believe one of their own might be guilty. It's easier to blame an outsider."

He stayed quiet for the rest of the ride, and Madelyn didn't press him. She sensed he needed his space.

Anyone would after a conversation like that.

When they pulled up to the marina, Zach spotted a group gathered around one of the piers. Madelyn walked beside him as he approached them. The crowd parted to let him through.

Zach peered down into the water. His stomach tightened when he saw the body of a man floating facedown.

A body. There was a body in the water. That was a little more than "something he'd want to see."

The man wore a flannel shirt, jeans and work boots. So unless he'd changed, he wasn't the man from the white truck they'd seen earlier. That had been his first thought. Did this man have anything to do with the fiasco taking place around here this week?

"We're going to need the state police out here," Zach mumbled. "Everyone, please take a step back."

He radioed Tyler before pulling out his camera and snapping some pictures. With the initial scene documented, Zach used a pole to flip the body over.

An unfamiliar face stared back. Zach stood, his hands on his hips as he studied the body. A bullet hole stained the man's chest, dark red liquid lining the edges.

The man had been shot.

This hadn't been an accidental death. The man hadn't fallen off a pier or been thrown from a boat or any of the other ways people might meet death around the water. This man had been murdered.

Zach turned toward the crowd. "Anyone recognize him?"

All around him, people shook their heads. There were

fishermen present—hobbyists and professionals—as well as boaters and dockworkers. None of them knew the man.

"Who found him?" Zach continued.

"I did, Chief." Rod stepped forward. "I was helping dock a boat when I saw something floating beneath the pier. I thought someone had dumped something in the bay—that's what it usually is. I couldn't believe my eyes when I realized it was a body. I called you right away."

"Anyone touch him?" Zach continued. He observed everyone's expressions, looking for a sign of deceit.

Again, the men around him shook their heads.

No one in particular looked uncomfortable. Most everyone at the marina was here, though there was another boat at the end of the docks unloading what appeared to be oysters. That crew continually looked over at the gathered crowd, as if wondering what was going on. Yet they continued to work.

Petty crimes had turned into violent crimes, and now there appeared to be a murderer at large.

It took an hour for the state police to show up and pull the body out of the water and onto the pier. Crime-scene tape had been pulled round the perimeter of the area, though Zach suspected there was little to preserve. Most, if not all, of the evidence had probably been washed out to sea at this point.

Not only did Zach have the mayor breathing down his neck, but now they had their first homicide here in Waterman's Reach in decades. Decades. Could things get any worse around here?

After slipping on some gloves, Zach reached into the man's pocket. A drape had been set up around the body to stop gawkers. Zach needed to see if he could find any identification. He pulled out a wallet, but there was nothing except a picture in the folds. Zach carefully pulled out the photo.

He sucked in a deep breath at the familiar face there. Madelyn.

Only this wasn't an ordinary photo. She wasn't smiling at the camera. No, in this photo Madelyn was climbing in her car, totally unaware the picture was being taken. It definitely appeared she was in the city. He spotted a parking meter in the corner of the photo. It had probably been taken in the summer based on the thin straps of the dress she was wearing.

This man was somehow connected with Madelyn and all of the eerie events that had been happening since she arrived in town. Had this man been watching her? Following her? Had he been hired to get rid of her?

Zach glanced up. Madelyn stood there with the rest of the crowd. When their gazes connected, she flinched. Did she sense that he'd discovered something of significance? Did she somehow know that she was connected with all of this?

Someone either wanted to kill Madelyn or to seriously hurt her. Neither option made him comfortable.

Zach glanced at the picture one more time before sliding it into a bag. He told Tyler to keep an eye on the scene while he pulled Madelyn aside.

"I know we've had this conversation before, but you might want to rethink staying here in Waterman's Reach," he told Madelyn. "This town isn't safe for you right now."

He had mixed feelings on the subject. At least when Madelyn was here, he could keep an eye on her. If she went back, Zach would be too far away to be much help. Truth was, he wanted her close. He didn't want her to leave. But her safety came first, before anything else.

"I'll be going back soon." The fading sunlight hit Madelyn's hair and made her look even more lovely than usual. But her eyes narrowed in curiosity and concern. "Why? What's going on?"

"I'm afraid that as long as you're here, you're in danger." Zach locked gazes with her, trying to drive home just how precarious things had become. "Madelyn, that body we found—"

He stopped, not wanting to finish. Up until this point, everything had simply been a threat. A dead body brought this investigation to an entirely new level.

"Yes?"

He shifted, rethinking how he wanted to word this. "That man we found in the water. Did you recognize him?"

She shook her head, looking surprised at his question. "I couldn't see him that well, but no. Why would you ask?"

"Think carefully." He studied her face, searching for any sign of deceit.

She squinted, as if Zach's questions were confusing her. "I'm positive that I don't know him. Why are you asking? Do you think I'm connected with him?"

He pulled out the photo and held it in front of her. "Your picture was in his pocket."

"What? That can't be right." Her voice rose in pitch. "Why in the world would my picture be in the man's pocket? I've never even seen him before."

Zach nodded solemnly, his expression remaining troubled. "That's what I'm trying to figure out."

Madelyn bit down on her lip and looked deep in thought. "I can assure you that I've never seen him before. I don't know how everything has turned into such a nightmare."

Zach squeezed her arm. "I'm going to be here a while. Why don't you go back to the bed-and-breakfast? There's nothing else you can do here."

She looked almost reluctant as she nodded. "I'll do that. I'll walk. I need the time to think anyway."

Zach watched her walk away, realizing the intricate web of clues surrounding this case grew more tangled by the moment.

EIGHTEEN

"Bad things are going to happen in life," the pastor said from the pulpit. "But that doesn't mean that God doesn't love you. In fact, the hard times should remind of how much He loves us. He can cover us with a peace that passes all understanding in the toughest moments of life."

Madelyn's rapt attention was on the pastor. It was as if he'd known she would be coming today and had catered this sermon just for her.

"Just remember, He's there holding your hand in the hardest moments of life. He's crying with you. He's wrapping His arms around you."

As he concluded his sermon, a tear slipped down Madelyn's cheek. She hadn't realized what a hole had been left in her life when she walked away from Jesus. But it had been there. She'd been trying desperately to fill it up with other things: men, her job, financial success. Nothing had worked.

Zach squeezed her shoulder. She'd noticed he'd slung his arm behind her during the sermon. Now she was forever grateful for his support. She was glad she'd come this morning, despite her misgivings.

I'm sorry, Lord, that I've tried to do all of this without You. I want to make things right.

She couldn't do this article. She had to trust her gut instinct and not rely on what Paula wanted. She'd known that all along, yet her internal compass had somehow gotten messed up.

Somehow, she had to find a way to come clean with Zach.

"I've got to drive up to Wachapreague. Would you like to come?" Zach asked as people began filing out.

"What's in Wachapreague?"

"A lead. A man went missing from the area last week. I want to see if he's possibly our John Doe."

She nodded. "Sure thing. Are you sure you want me with you during the investigation?"

"I don't have the resources to plant an officer outside the B and B to guard you 24-7. So if you want to come along, I don't think anyone would have a problem with it." He plucked a hair from her shoulder, then pushed the rest of the strands behind her ear. The action seemed so warm, so intimate that her cheeks flushed.

"Okay."

"We figured out who that white truck belonged to. A man named Jeffery Severs."

She craned her neck in confusion. "I've never heard of him."

"It was stolen last week from his home in Baltimore."

She processed what he said. Had she heard him correctly? "So you think trouble followed me from Baltimore?"

"I had suspected as much. And that's how it appears right now."

She felt herself go pale and crossed her arms, the day cooler than usual. She wished she'd brought a jacket. "Why wait until I get here? Things seemed fine up in Baltimore."

"That's a great question."

Once they were safely inside his car and cruising down the road, he stole a glance her way. "You looked a little emotional in church this morning."

She shrugged, feeling like the tears could come back at any minute. "I just realized how meaningless life has been this last decade without Jesus in it. I blamed God for what happened to my parents. I wanted to be angry with someone. Maybe two someones."

"Two?"

"God and the police officer who hit them."

"It was a tragedy what happened to them, Madelyn. No one can deny that." He reached over and grabbed her hand.

Such a simple action brought her immense comfort, though. "It was tragic. But it was even more tragic that I let that come between me and my faith. My parents raised me better than that."

"Yet faith has to be about more than how your parents raise you. It has to be personal."

"It will be now. If God can forgive me for turning my back on Him."

"All you have to do is ask." As she thought about his words, they pulled to a stop in another seaside fishing community. Maybe they'd get some answers here.

If she wanted to remain alive, she hoped that was true.

They'd hit pay dirt while talking to a woman who owned a kayak-excursion business in Wachapreague. The woman had identified the dead man as thirty-four-year-old Bobby Wilson. Bobby, a part-time fisherman, had been last seen six days ago. He was supposed to head up to Baltimore to purchase a boat, but he hadn't been seen or heard from since then.

Zach glanced at Madelyn as they walked back to his car. "How do you feel about taking a trip up to your neck of the woods?"

She shrugged. "I'm along for the ride. Whatever you want. You really think this guy is connected to everything that's happened lately?"

"Until we can rule him out, it remains a possibility. I mean really, we have no discernible motive here. Unless you can think of a reason why someone wants to kill you."

"I can't."

"So until we can figure that out, everyone remains a suspect." And he did mean everyone—Chief Watson, Mayor Alan, even Rod. He had to find the real culprit.

Madelyn paused by the car and nodded toward the convenience store across the lot. "Mind if I grab a water before we hit the road?"

"Go right ahead."

After she disappeared into the store, he climbed into his car and sat back, trying to clear his head a moment. Something began ringing. Was that a cell phone? He looked down and saw an illuminated screen by the gearshift. He picked up the device, and a picture of a blonde woman with the name *Paula* at the bottom of the screen appeared.

Paula? Why did her picture and name sound familiar?

He couldn't pinpoint it exactly, but her photo remained in the back of his mind as Madelyn climbed back in.

She handed him a water also. "Let's go!"

He shoved the thought from his mind and started down the road. Maybe the woman just had one of those faces. If not, it would hit him eventually.

As they got closer and closer to Baltimore, his stomach contorted. He hadn't been back since he left. In fact, he tried to avoid it. He could live with a ruined reputation, but that didn't mean he liked it.

He'd become a villain after that night. He'd gotten death threats. He'd had to move out of his home when people repeatedly vandalized it.

While most on the police force seemed to still support him, some thought he should have resigned immediately. He'd hoped justice and fairness would prevail, but when it became obvious that his presence was only making things worse, he'd decided to step down.

"What are you thinking about?" Madelyn asked.

He considered his words. "About how hard it can be to go back."

"I realize that Baltimore has a lot of bad memories for you."

He nodded slowly, somberly. "I guess you weren't there when all of that went down."

She shook her head. "I only moved here a year ago. I was in Pennsylvania before that."

"I was tried and found guilty by the media before a full investigation could even start." Images flashed in his head. Reporters dug up every piece of dirt they could find. Most they'd exaggerated. A few so-called facts were plain made-up based on hearsay.

They'd interviewed anyone who had a reason to dislike him. Family members of people—criminals—who had been put away for life. The officer who'd lost a promotion when Zach had been made detective instead of him.

In the process, they'd forgotten about all the good he'd done. The people's lives he'd saved. The ways he'd sacrificed much of his personal life for what he considered to be his God-given calling.

"That had to be difficult." A look of anguish crossed her features.

Was it because Madelyn was a member of the media? Did she understand what it was like to be on the other side? To be desperate for a story? For a headline?

He couldn't see her as that type. In fact, being a travel writer seemed to fit her personality well. She was spunky, but not pushy or hungry for attention, no matter the cost to others.

"The media can be cruel." He stole another glance at her. "But you don't seem like that."

Her cheeks flushed. "I don't?"

"No, you have honest eyes."

She fiddled with her fingers in her lap, almost appearing embarrassed. "Thank you."

There was no time to talk about this anymore right now. They pulled to a stop at the marina where Bobby Wilson had supposedly last been seen. Zach braced himself to face his past.

"His name isn't listed anywhere at this marina," a gruff man told them. "Nor do I know of anyone selling any boats here. I'm usually privy to information like that. I like to be in the know about what's going on."

It wasn't really surprising, Madelyn thought. There had already been so many lies and untruths. Bobby had used buying a boat as an excuse to come here.

Madelyn glanced around at the marina. She'd never been here before. This one was actually on the outskirts of town and not at the main harbor. But, with probably forty slips, it was much larger than those she'd seen on the Eastern Shore.

Large boats waited at the pier, which indicated deep waters lapped against the bulkhead. However, it was the same bay here as in Waterman's Reach. Right now, they were on the north peak of the Chesapeake Bay. It was hard to believe the body of water stretched so far.

"Zach Davis?"

Zach and Madelyn both turned toward the voice. A police officer stood there, a questioning look in his eyes. The man was short but burly with close-cropped hair and a ruddy complexion. Madelyn braced herself for the worst.

"Phil Madison," Zach said.

A smile broke across the officer's face. "It's been a long time. How's it going?"

"It's going," Zach said, his voice warming. "How are you doing?"

"We're hanging in. It's been a long time. I wasn't sure if I'd ever see you back up this way again."

"Just doing some legwork for a case I'm working on down in Waterman's Reach."

Phil leaned closer. "You know that heroin we were trying to get off the streets?"

"I can't forget it."

"It's still being used around here. We've had thirty-two other inner-city youth who've died with it in their blood. We still can't pinpoint where it's originated. Can you believe it? After all these years and still no leads."

"I can believe it. When someone's making that kind of money, they're going to stay quiet about it rather than risk their livelihood." Zach frowned.

"We have a task force together trying to nail these guys, but there are so many hoops that have to be jumped through. Sometimes it doesn't seem like we're ever going to figure it out."

"I hope you do. Someone's gotten away with this for too long now."

"You look good, man," Phil said. His gaze turned to Madelyn and he nodded politely.

Zach shifted and touched Madelyn's shoulder. "Excuse my manners. Phil, this is Madelyn."

"Nice to meet you," Phil said as they shook hands. "I'm glad you found someone, Zach. No one at the department ever really liked Julia."

Zach opened his mouth, surely about to correct him about his relationship status with Madelyn. Before he could, Phil waved to someone in the distance.

"I've got to get back to patrol. But great to see you, Zach."

Zach continued asking men along the docks if they'd seen Bobby Wilson before. Madelyn walked alongside the water, her thoughts swirling inside.

How did Bobby fit in with all of this? Why was her picture in his pocket? There were so many loose ends and so few answers.

As she paused to stare over the water, she sensed movement beside her. The next thing she knew, something hit her shoulder. A man. Shoving her.

She felt herself falling toward the deep water below.

NINETEEN

Zach turned and saw Madelyn falling. The next instant, her head hit the side of the dock before her body plunged into the water.

A man sprinted away in the distance.

"Someone get him!" he yelled, hoping Phil was still close enough to hear. Zach had to help Madelyn.

He jumped into the water, his heart pounding at the thought of something happening to her.

The bay surrounded him, took his breath away. The water was a good twelve feet deep here, at least. He'd seen Madelyn hit her head on the pier on the way down, and he feared the worst.

The water was thick, almost dirty from the grime of ship repair and pollution. He opened his eyes, hoping the sunlight was strong enough to break through the murkiness. His eyes stung as the liquid hit.

He could barely see his hand in front of his face.

His lungs squeezed, in want of air. He had to stay under for as long as he could, though.

He knew Madelyn had gone under in this general area. She couldn't be too far.

Despite his burning lungs, he pushed himself down deeper.

There! Was that the faint impression of a hand? It was merely a shadow, a glimpse, a hunch, for that matter. But it was all he had to go on.

His lungs screamed now, but he wasn't going to give up. He couldn't.

He grabbed the fingers that almost seemed to be reaching for him and tugged.

Madelyn's motionless face came into view. Her eyes were closed, her hair fanned out in the water, her body limp with unconsciousness. And she looked nearly lifeless beneath the water.

With a spike of adrenaline, he pulled her to the surface, gasping for air as soon as his head emerged. He dragged her toward the pier, her head sagging against his shoulder.

A group of onlookers on the pier hauled Madelyn out of the water and onto the rough wood.

Phil was among the crowd. He took charge as Zach dragged himself out of the water. Phil turned Madelyn onto her side, pounding her back as he tried to get water out of her lungs.

Once out of the water, Zach caught his breath. But only a moment—long enough to steady the spinning in his head— before rushing to Madelyn. As he knelt beside her, he began praying.

Lord, please be with her. Clear her lungs. Heal her.

Phil continued doing CPR.

Zach's prayers became more fervent as the minutes ticked past. Every second mattered in situations like this.

Finally, Madelyn coughed, water sputtering out of her mouth as she did. Her body jerked with the motion. But she was moving. She was breathing.

She was alive.

Thank goodness she was alive.

Because that had been close. Too close.

* * *

Madelyn had been fussing with the doctors to let her go, insisting she was fine. But they wanted to keep an eye on her for a couple of hours longer because she'd hit her head on the way down.

She shivered every time she thought about how close that had been. If Zach hadn't been there... She shuddered. She'd come a little too near to death. Someone had made it clear they wanted her dead.

She pressed her head back into her pillow, wanting to both shut out the memories and to analyze them. Part of her only wanted to pretend all of this was just a nightmare that she would wake up from. It was obvious the stakes had risen. This was no longer a matter of scaring Madelyn away. It was a matter of killing her.

Someone knocked on her door before stepping into her room. Zach. He wore jeans and a Henley, and he'd never looked so handsome. Her throat went dry at the sight of him.

"I was giving a report to the police while the doctor checked you out," he said, stopping by her bed. "Sorry I wasn't here sooner."

"No need to apologize. You did save me. Again."

"I'm just glad you're okay." His hand covered hers and caused her heart to lurch into her throat.

He had such a strong effect on her—more than any man ever had. That realization scared her.

She forced herself to focus. "Did they catch the guy who pushed me?"

He shook his head. "Phil went after him, but he had too much of a head start. The man jumped into a truck that had been waiting for him. We're running the plates under the assumption that it was probably stolen."

She frowned as she let that sink in. "Someone must be following our every move."

"I'd venture to say you're correct."

She let her head fall back against the pillow, suddenly weary and spent. Her assignment had seemed so simple. How had it turned into all of this? "It just proves that I'm not going to be safe. Anywhere. These guys aren't going to stop until I'm out of commission."

Zach pulled up a chair beside her. When he sat down, his hand covered hers again. "Madelyn, can you think of any reason why someone would want to hurt you? Any reason at all? I know we've been over this before, but maybe something new surfaced in your mind."

She shook her head, pushing aside the realization that Zach was the only one with a strong enough motive. He obviously wasn't responsible. Remorse filled her at the thought.

"I've thought about it from every angle possible," she said. "It just doesn't make sense. First those stupid oysters were stolen. Then someone broke into my house, shot at me, left me stranded on an island and now this. This person doesn't just want to scare me. They're determined to finish the job."

"I agree that it's puzzling. But if there's anything else you can think of… Anything at all. I've mentioned this before, but maybe this all ties in some way with your journalism."

She sighed. "My last article was about a mountain resort in Pennsylvania. I can hardly imagine why someone would be mad about it. There was nothing controversial about the piece. In fact, I got a thank-you letter from several of the business owners, telling me I'd helped boost tourism in the town. They practically wanted to make me an honorary citizen."

"Ok. This all started when you were assigned to do an article on Waterman's Reach. So maybe someone is afraid you'll discover something they don't want uncovered."

His words made her tense all over. Zach's name came to her mind again. He was the only person with motive.

But Zach had been with her during many of these incidents. He couldn't be behind them. Besides, he'd saved her life.

If he really was somehow responsible, he would have let someone go through with the crime. But instead, he'd stopped this person or people time and time again.

But if not Zach then who?

The question was unnerving.

Three hours later, Madelyn was released from the hospital. She wore some old sweatpants and a T-shirt—not the most flattering outfit. She definitely wasn't dressed for success, but at least she had been able to wash the bay water out of her hair and felt clean.

Zach helped her to his Bronco, and they climbed inside. Night had already fallen. It was hard to believe that just this morning she'd been in church yearning to be close to God again. It seemed like a week had passed already.

Instead of driving straight to Waterman's Reach, Zach pulled off the highway a good thirty minutes early. Madelyn didn't even bother to ask where he was going, but she figured he had a good reason for his actions.

Unless he wanted to kill her.

She shook her head at the thought. A few days ago, she might have believed it. Not anymore.

Finally, he pulled to a stop in front of a sandy beach surrounded by nothing but trees on both sides and put the car in Park.

"What's this?" Madelyn stared at the land, wishing it wasn't so dark so she could see more.

"This is…mine."

She blinked. "Yours? Really?"

He nodded. "I bought it about five years ago when I

thought I was going to get married. I thought it would be a nice place to put down roots and build a house one day." There was a certain melancholy undertone to his voice.

"Then she broke things off? That had to hurt."

"To add insult to injury, she turned on me. Started doing interviews with the media and claiming that I'd been acting funny lately. Secretive. That was almost worse—being betrayed by someone you love hurt entirely more than being betrayed by people who only wanted a face and name to put the blame on."

Guilt pounded at her temples. Zach had suffered a great pain at the hands of someone he'd loved. Madelyn was about to betray him also. He didn't love her, but he was starting to trust her. How could she do this?

"I'm sorry, Zach," she finally croaked.

"Maybe it was for the best. I've learned that setbacks are usually just God's way of redirecting us."

"I like that." Was God redirecting her right now? She'd have to think about that later.

"I don't talk about this much, but that gang member who was killed in the drug bust? I knew him."

Her pulse raced. Was this the confession that Paula had hoped for? "Did you?"

"He was paired with me for a mentoring program about two years before that drug bust went down. It was an initiative to make cops seem more like friends and less like enemies. You know, it wanted inner-city kids to make that connection while they were young. Anyway, I was paired with Mario. We'd play basketball together and got together to talk at least once a week."

"Wow, I'm sorry to hear that." Her gut twisted. How did that letter fit in?

"I tried to get him to turn from his life of drugs. I saw the path he was headed down. But he wouldn't listen. He said I was just like every other cop he'd met. That's what made that whole fiasco even harder."

So that's what the letter had been about! She'd known there had to be a good explanation. Zach was innocent all along.

He snapped out of the moment of reflection and turned toward her, a touch of hope in his eyes. "Want to see it?"

"Of course."

They climbed out and walked across the sandy grass until they reached the shore. A lone park bench sat there. She took a seat and absorbed the moment.

This location was far enough away from the lights of the city that the stars shone brightly above. And the moon hovered high in the sky, reflecting on the glassy water. Waves gently lapped the shoreline with a whooshing sound while insects buzzed from the woods in the distance.

When Madelyn closed her eyes, she couldn't hear the traffic like she did at home. It seemed…peaceful.

"I think this would be a great place for a house."

"Me, too. This is where I came when I needed to clear my head. It's tranquil and makes me feel like I can breathe." He paused. "I just put it on the market. So someone else will get to use this. Hopefully, it will become a part of their dreams."

"I'm sorry, Zach." She squeezed his hand, knowing how hard it was when dreams died.

He shook his head, holding tightly to her hand. "Don't be sorry. It's the way life works sometimes."

"Any reason in particular you wanted me to see this?"

He shifted beside her, closer than she's realized. She didn't mind, though. "Would you believe me if I said I didn't know?"

His eyes mesmerized her, and she couldn't look away. "Sure, I'd believe it."

"It's just that in the craziness of this past week, being

around you has been one of the only reprieves I've felt. You've surprised me. I thought you were going to be this big-city, career-driven reporter who didn't care about anything or anyone. That you'd be all about your byline, designers' clothes and getting ahead."

Her cheeks flushed. She wasn't done surprising him yet. She needed to tell him the truth. But the words seemed to lodge in her throat.

"You've surprised me also," she finally said. She lingered between being the delight of the moment and the harsh reality of the inevitable time when she'd have to admit the truth. It had been so long since she'd wanted to be swept away. She didn't want to let that go.

"Madelyn…" he started.

Before he could say anything else, their eyes met. His gaze went to her lips.

Madelyn sucked in a shallow breath, hardly able to breathe. They both seemed to intrinsically lean toward each other. The scent of his woodsy cologne filled her nostrils again, and she wanted to bury herself in the smell.

Tentatively, their lips brushed. She wasn't sure who initiated it, but neither pulled away.

They paused as if testing how receptive the other was. Madelyn could feel Zach's heart pounding beneath her hand. Zach's hand slipped around the back of her neck, and he pulled her toward him.

She could hardly breathe, hardly move, hardly wanted the moment to end.

"On second thought, I know why I brought you here," he whispered, his face only inches from hers.

"Why's that?"

"Because when I saw you go in the water today, I couldn't deny any longer how much I was starting to care about you."

She had no words. Instead, she leaned in for another kiss. Something about it just felt right.

But she was going to have to tell Zach the truth. Tonight. That thought made her stomach churn with dread.

TWENTY

Guilt pounded at Madelyn. On their ride home, she hadn't been able to speak the words she needed to say to Zach. Every time she'd opened her mouth to confess, nothing came out. The truth made her hopes want to crash. Made her want to cry. Made her desperate to turn back time.

All she could think about was how she was ruining something beautiful. Something for which she'd been looking for a long time. That thought made her heart ache.

What if Zach didn't forgive her? What if he never gazed at her again with the same look of affection in his eyes?

She had some other pressing questions. What was she going to tell Paula? Would she have a job after she refused to write this article? If not with East Coast International, where could she work?

She had no support system to fall back on. No family to live with if she ran out of money. No backup plan if she no longer had a paycheck.

There were so many uncertainties that she couldn't sleep that night. Instead, she tossed and turned. One moment, she replayed their kiss with bliss-like delight. The next minute, she envisioned herself telling Zach the truth, and her very bones ached with dread. In between those thoughts, she relived being pushed into the water. Nothing felt simple or safe.

Finally, bright and early the next morning, she pushed herself out of bed. She had to get this over with. She had to tell Zach the truth.

Lord, I know it's been a while. But if there's ever been a time that I've needed You, it's now. I've made a lot of mistakes. I've been selfish. But I want to change. I want to make things right. I desperately need Your wisdom.

Just as Madelyn threw her feet over the edge of the bed, her phone buzzed on the nightstand. She glanced at her alarm clock. It was only 7:32 a.m. Who would be texting her at this hour?

Wiping the sleep out of her eyes, she stared at the screen. The text was from another reporter at East Coast International. It simply read, "Good job. This is your moment."

Good job? Good job with what?

A feeling of anxiety mixed with curiosity. She hurried across the room and pulled out her laptop, the sinking feeling in her stomach growing by the second. Her hands trembled as she typed in the web address for ECI.

There on the home page was the picture she'd sent to Paula. The one of Zach exchanging an envelope with Milton. The headline read, Former Baltimore Detective Takes Hush Money for Drug Trafficking.

No, no, no!

Madelyn quickly scanned the article. Paragraph after paragraph basically accused Zach of taking hush money while allowing heroin to be smuggled up to Baltimore. It also accused Milton of being involved and turning a blind eye to the exchanges down at the docks.

People had been interviewed, including someone from the Baltimore PD who had been quoted as saying Zach had always been out for himself.

Nothing had been left out. According to the exposé, Zach had taken the job in Waterman's Reach so he could keep a better eye on the operations taking place in the town. He had a secret account where he was funneling his profits until he could make a run for it. Anyone who got in his way was killed. Including Bobby Wilson.

Then her eyes zeroed in on the byline.

Madelyn Sawyer.

She closed her eyes, panic shaking her entire body. How was she going to correct this? How could Paula do something like this?

She had to talk to Paula. Now. Maybe if she could reason with her she'd take the article down before it did any damage. Before anyone saw it. She knew it was a long shot, but she was desperate.

She dialed Paula's cell. The phone rang and rang and rang.

What? Paula always picked up. She practically had her phone glued to her hand.

Madelyn hung up and tried again. Still no answer.

She had to talk to Zach. Now. Before he saw the article. Maybe—just maybe—she could make things right.

She threw on some clothes and jumped into her car, no time to waste.

Zach had awoken early to start his day. He had a lot to do and no time to waste. With every second that ticked past, there was a killer out there and the chances of Madelyn being hurt again only increased. He couldn't let that happen.

He needed to review all of his notes and try to make a connection between the various crimes that had occurred recently. There was a link—he just had to find it.

He still needed to speak with Levi Watson today. It wouldn't be pretty. It might even cost him his job. But he had to follow that lead. It was his duty.

No one else was in the office when Zach arrived before

the sun rose, and that was fine by him. The quiet would give him more time to himself.

What had he been thinking last night when he kissed Madelyn? He hadn't planned it. Not really. But he didn't regret it either.

Since Madelyn had come into town, his life had been turned upside down. He couldn't stop thinking about her smile, her touch, her inquisitiveness. He hadn't felt like this since Julia. And if he was honest, he hadn't even felt quite this strongly about Julia. The two of them had had a lot of fun together, but when the going got tough, it had proven that their relationship was just fun.

It felt different with Madelyn. So different that he didn't want it to end. There was a certain depth to their conversations. A certain connection on a deeper level.

He realized, however, that she had to go back home soon. He didn't know what that would mean for their relationship, but he hoped they could figure it out together.

He rubbed his eyes and turned away from his notes for a moment. He needed to look at his emails and see if any new leads had come in.

The first subject line he spotted made him pause. "You have to see this article."

He squinted. It was from Chris, his friend with the Coast Guard.

As he clicked on the link his friend shared, his gut tightened with anticipation. What could this be about?

His eyes widened when he saw his picture. He was giving an envelope to Milton Johnson. The headline read "Former Baltimore Detective Takes Hush Money for Drug Trafficking."

His eyes traveled down the page.

The byline read Madelyn Sawyer. Had she been here in Waterman's Reach to scope him out this whole time?

Had the travel article just been a cover story? That's how it appeared.

Just as he finished reading the article, he heard a gasp behind him.

"I can explain," someone said. "Please."

Madelyn. How dare she show her face around here after writing this article?

Zach rose from his seat, a mix of accusation and hurt in his eyes. "Is this why you really came to Waterman's Reach?"

"Zach, I didn't write that article." Her voice sounded desperate, high-pitched.

He scowled, a steel guard coming down around him. He'd been wrong to trust her. "Let me guess—you didn't take that picture either."

She nibbled on her lip a moment before frowning. "I did, but—"

He stepped closer, righteous indignation rushing through him. "That's what this was all about all along, wasn't it? You wanted to get close to me in order to dig up dirt, write the story of your career and bring me down. I fell for it hook, line and sinker."

"Please, I can explain."

He glowered down at her. "You have one minute."

"Originally, I was sent here to find out information about you. But I couldn't do it, Zach. I didn't think you were guilty."

He didn't move, didn't give any indication he believed her or even wanted to believe her. There were too many holes in her story. "How'd that article get published then?"

"My editor must have done it—"

"And used your byline?" His gaze seared into hers.

She nodded and lowered her head. "I don't know why she did it. She's not answering her phone."

He shook his head. "Madelyn, I trusted you. I wanted

to see where the future might go with you as a part of it. But now I can see that was a mistake."

"Zach—"

He sliced his hand through the air. "I have nothing else to say. This would probably be a good time for you to get out of town. I'm sure I'll be following soon, after Mayor Alan and everyone else in town sees this piece."

She reached for him. "Zach, I never meant for any of this to happen. Please. You've got to believe me."

He turned his back. "Goodbye, Madelyn."

Madelyn felt her shoulders sagging as she walked back into the bed-and-breakfast. That couldn't have gone any worse. She'd made an absolute disaster of things. And, other than the fact that she didn't write that article, she couldn't blame Zach for being upset.

As soon as she spotted Eva, Madelyn knew she'd seen the article, too. There was no denying the anger in her gaze, in the set of her shoulders, in her stiff movements.

"How could you?" she demanded.

Madelyn shook her head, knowing she deserved whatever came her way. "I'm sorry, Eva."

"Do you have any idea what was in that envelope?"

"I don't."

"Money. Zach was paying out of his own pocket for your stay here. He knew we were struggling to make ends meet and wanted to help out."

The guilt hit her even harder. Her own preconceived notions had led to her undoing. "I had no idea."

"All you had to do was ask and we would have told you, even if it wasn't your business. The chief is a good man. I don't know who you think you are, coming in here and fooling everyone in town."

"I never intended for things to happen this way. I'll get

my stuff and leave." Sadness crushed her heart. "I truly am sorry."

"Sorry isn't good enough right now. People are going to think my husband has something to do with drug running. Any hopes we had of making something of this bed-and-breakfast are ruined."

"I'll make things right."

Eva shook her head. "The only way you can make things right is by getting out of here. I don't think anyone in town will want to see your face again."

Madelyn wanted to argue, but Eva was probably right. Madelyn had done irreparable harm to the lives of more than one person.

Once she left, maybe all the crime would go with her. Maybe she'd truly been the source of all of these problems. But the trouble wouldn't end for Zach, would it? He'd probably lose his job. Would an investigation open up on him again? Would he be able to find a new town and work there as law enforcement?

Her head pounded at the thoughts. How could she make things right? How could she undo all of the wrongs she'd done?

As she threw clothes into her suitcase, she tried to call Paula again. Why wasn't her editor answering the phone? Madelyn even tried her office and home number. There was no answer at either.

Something wasn't right.

How was Madelyn going to fix this? The task seemed insurmountable.

She had to think of something. She'd drive up to Baltimore and confront Paula face-to-face if she had to. She'd demand a retraction. She'd become part of the news, if that's what she had to do in order to have her byline removed.

She closed her suitcase, and despite the fact that Zach had paid for her stay, she left a check on the dresser for her stay here and clamored back downstairs. Eva was nowhere to be seen, so she slipped out the back door and put everything in her car. She knew there was nowhere in town she could go and be welcome. Besides, she had to confront what she'd done head-on. That meant confronting Paula.

Only ten minutes on the highway, she heard a pop. Her shoulders drooped.

What now?

As the car began bumping, she realized she had a flat tire. Wasn't that just great? The timing couldn't be any worse.

As she pulled to the side of the road, she glanced in her rearview mirror.

A police cruiser had pulled up behind her. Zach?

Her hopes deflated as she realized it was Tyler.

She braced herself for another confrontation.

TWENTY-ONE

Zach expected a call from the mayor at any time. Before that happened, he wanted to speak with former chief Watson.

His blood still boiled as he thought about Madelyn's betrayal. How could he have fallen for her act? He'd prided himself in being smarter than that. But she'd pulled the wool over his eyes.

Anger simmered inside him at the thought. Not only had she tricked him, she'd set him up. Was she the one behind the acts happening in town? If so, she would have to have been working with someone, since the incidents had been against her. But why? Had she been trying to earn his trust and sympathy?

He didn't know what to think anymore. But he had a shooter in town, a dead body and general mayhem. He wanted answers now more than ever.

He also needed to figure out who was responsible for importing those drugs into the harbor. His best guess right now was Levi. If there was one thing Zach had to do before his time here was up, it was talk to the man. He had nothing to lose anymore.

Zach knocked on the door, and Levi answered a moment later. As soon as the former chief spotted him, his eyes narrowed. He'd already seen the news article. No doubt most people in town had. Gossip like that spread like wildfire in these small communities.

"I'm surprised you're still showing your face around here."

Zach resisted the urge to scowl. "Levi, I need to know if you tampered with Ernie's boat."

His eyes darkened. "What do you mean? I told you I forgot my fishing rod."

"Are you sure you didn't tamper with his boat in an effort to run Madelyn Sawyer out of town?"

"Now why would I do that?"

"Maybe you were afraid she'd uncover something about you, something that you don't want the citizens of Waterman's Reach to know."

Levi shook his head. "Are you trying to get fired? Because whether the mayor likes me or not, he doesn't want to get on my bad side. He'll fire you in a second."

Zach stepped closer. "I think you're up to no good here in town, Levi. You've wanted nothing more than to make me look bad since the day I arrived."

"Why would you say that?"

"You're the one who slit my tires and knocked down my mailbox, aren't you?"

He raised his chin defiantly. "You'll never prove it."

Zach couldn't let this go yet. "Just because Tyler didn't get the job?"

The man's lip twitched upward with disgust. "He deserved the position."

"The mayor obviously didn't agree."

"The mayor doesn't know what he's doing. He's hated me since I stole his girlfriend back in high school."

"Are you the one who left the blood in my house? Who shot at me?"

He scoffed. "Now you're insulting me. I wouldn't be that stupid."

Zach lowered his voice, trying a different approach. "Levi, it's important that I figure out what's going on before someone else ends up dead."

His speech didn't work on Levi. The man shook his head. "I don't even know why you're asking me these questions. Tyler already came by and got a statement from me about the boat incident. Don't you trust my nephew?"

"That's funny. I never sent him here." Why had Tyler come? It seemed odd that he'd take that initiative himself.

"Sounds like there's a lack of leadership down at the department then," Levi said. "I never had any rogue officers when I was on the job."

Before Zach could ask any more questions, Levi slammed the door.

Tyler. Could Tyler be involved in all of this somehow?

Where was his officer now exactly? He hadn't checked in this morning as normal, but Zach had been too preoccupied to notice.

A gnawing feeling began in his gut.

Zach needed to find Tyler. Now.

"I was patrolling the area and saw you had a flat." Tyler leaned in Madelyn's window.

"I guess that works in my favor," she said, surprised that he was being as kind to her as he was, since Zach was Tyler's boss. She figured he would be outraged for his brother in blue.

"I can help you change it. If you just want to step out of the car."

"Thank you. I appreciate it."

With trembling hands, she stepped from her sedan and popped the trunk. Apparently, Fisher's Auto Repair had patched her spare while the car was in the shop. The tire no longer looked lopsided and uneven. "I hope it will make it to Baltimore."

"I'm not sure about that. But maybe you can at least make it to a mechanic." Tyler pulled the tire out, as well as the jack and wrenches. "I heard about the article."

Madelyn crossed her arms. She figured it would come up. She wasn't really in the mood to talk, though. She just wanted to get out of town and away from all the damage she'd done. She needed some space so she could figure out how to make things right.

"It's a long story."

"I don't blame you for writing it," he said, slipping the jack under her car.

"Why's that?" Some kind of emotion pinched at her spine. Fear? Instinct?

"I've known the chief was up to something for a while. I just haven't been able to prove it."

Her spine pinched harder. "What do you mean?"

"I've suspected Zach was involved in some illegal activities. I also have proof that he's the one who's been trying to kill you."

Madelyn shivered. "Proof?"

Tyler abandoned the jack in order to stand and pull out his phone. "I found this photo at the marina."

Madelyn stared at the phone. It was a picture of a man who appeared to be Zach, his back to the camera, at the marina near Ernie's boat.

She let his implications sink in. "You think *Zach* sabotaged Ernie's boat? That's crazy."

"He also has deep connections. He has a whole network of drug dealers at his disposal. Maybe he didn't leave you stranded, but that doesn't mean he's not responsible."

"He's the one who saved me that day on the water. What sense would it make for him to be the one who also put me in danger?"

Tyler shrugged, dragging his shoulder up to his ear as he pulled her flat tire off. "Maybe he wanted to look like the good guy. Then he'd win the trust of the town's people. You know how it works."

She stepped back and shook her head, unable to believe it. She'd seen Zach's eyes—there was no deceit there. "That can't be true."

"Think about it. Zach could have hired someone to do his dirty work. Make himself look good. Run you out of town before you destroyed his reputation."

"He wouldn't do that." Madelyn's thoughts clashed inside her head.

"He's going to be really mad when it sinks in just how much you ruined. His whole operation is over now."

Fear flooded her. Something wasn't right. Her instincts were screaming for her attention.

"There you go. Your tire is all fixed." Tyler stood and wiped his hands on a rag. "This should get you down the road."

Suddenly, she couldn't wait to leave. "Thank you. I appreciate your help."

At that moment, she glanced down at her tire. At Tyler standing beside it.

His shoes.

Those were the same black shoes she'd seen on the night she'd been pushed into the shed. The image of them was ingrained in her memory. Tyler was behind the threats on her life.

Fear tried to seize her. She couldn't let that happen. She had to get out of here.

Now.

She started toward the driver's side door when Tyler grabbed her arm.

"Too bad you won't be making it back to Baltimore," he muttered.

Her blood felt ice-cold as fear seized her. "What do you mean?"

"I'm not finished with you yet." Before she could scream, he swiped his gun around her temple.

Then everything went black.

Zach raced to Tyler's house, desperate for answers. He pounded on the door, but no one answered. Where was the officer? Zach had called Lynn on the way here, and she hadn't heard from Tyler yet. She'd also informed him that the mayor was at the office waiting for him, and he didn't look happy. The mayor was the least of his concerns at the moment.

Zach twisted the door handle and, to his surprise, it turned. With only a touch of contemplation, he pushed the door open and stepped inside Tyler's place. He'd never been inside before, and he didn't want to overstep his boundaries. But he had to find some answers.

He paced into the living room and glanced around. Everything appeared normal. Hand-me-down furniture, minimal decorations, this morning's breakfast dishes left in the sink.

He paused by a bookshelf in the living room, squinting at one of the loose pictures there. His throat tightened.

It was a picture of a man who looked strikingly like Zach. He was standing beside Ernie's boat, and the date on the bottom matched the date Ernie's boat was tampered with. Someone was setting him up to look guilty.

All the facts were colliding together in his mind and forming a disturbing picture. Were the answers right under his nose this whole time? How could Zach have not seen it?

Where exactly was Madelyn now? He needed to find her. Right away.

He stepped into the backyard, desperate to make sure he wasn't missing anything here. As he stepped onto the deck, his shin knocked into a cooler.

Oysters spilled onto the wood. As he reached down

to pick one up, he saw plastic peeking out from one of the shells.

His heart raced.

He pried the shell the rest of the way open. A bag of white powder had been stuffed inside.

Suddenly, he knew exactly how these drug dealers had gotten away with their crime for so long. Tyler had been behind it. He'd used the town's oyster industry as a front to transport drugs up the East Coast, and he'd used his position on the police force to keep the operation hidden.

Tyler.

He shook his head, unable to believe it. He must have used those barrier islands as a meeting point with his supplier. The drugs probably came from the Middle East, were shipped into Mexico or Central America, and then they were brought here. Maybe even while Tyler was on patrol.

What if Tyler had thought Madelyn was in town to uncover the truth about his drug operation? He could have tried to scare her off by following her, by threatening her on the first night here. Then he'd escalated by shooting at her and sabotaging the boat.

In the meantime, Tyler would try to frame this all on Zach.

Now that the truth was out about Madelyn's article, would she still be in danger? Zach would guess yes. Tyler was going to finish this and make it look like Zach had gone off the deep end and killed Madelyn as revenge for exposing him.

He had to find Tyler. And Madelyn.

There was no time to waste.

TWENTY-TWO

When Madelyn came to, darkness surrounded her.

She gasped as the details of what had happened rushed back to her. Tyler. He was behind all of this. He'd knocked her out. He'd probably been the one who'd shot at her. Broke into her house. Maybe even pushed her off that pier. But why?

And where was she now?

She pushed back her panic and tried to absorb her surroundings a moment. There was a soft hum. Occasional bumps. Scratchy fabric brushed her cheek. An oily scent filled the air.

The trunk, she realized.

She was in the back of Tyler's car, and they were heading down the road. Her hands and feet were bound. Tape had been placed over her mouth.

Where was he taking her? Would anyone realize that she was gone?

Zach… Zach might realize it, but he probably wouldn't care if he ever saw her again. In fact, she was probably the last person he wanted to think about.

Paula…well, she'd betrayed Madelyn in order to further her own career. An exposé like the one she'd written would skyrocket East Coast International's credibility.

Paula wasn't likely to be sending out a search party any time soon. Her number one priority was herself.

This could very well be the way everything ended for Madelyn. She'd been alone in the world for the past ten years, and she would die alone and without anyone to care.

That thought caused an ache to form in her chest.

No, that wasn't true. Jesus. She had Jesus. He cared. He was watching out for her now, no matter what happened.

You've always been there for me, haven't You? Even when I haven't acknowledged it? Even when I've pushed You away?

The thought somehow brought comfort to her.

If she got out of this alive, she was going to make some major changes in her life.

At one time, she'd wanted to be just like Paula. Not anymore. Paula was selfish, living only for herself and for the treasures this world afforded. Madelyn had known of a deeper purpose and a more authentic meaning in life. She knew what it was like to love, to look out for others, to listen to more than what the world and society threw at her.

Her parents had taught her those things. Things like putting other people first. Loving the unlovable. Sacrificing your own desires for the greater good. Madelyn was so sorry she'd forgotten. Her life had been so empty for all of these years without her moral compass. Without being grounded. Without a hope that went beyond what she could see.

I want to change things, Lord. I want to be better.

Just then, the car rumbled, as if driving over gravel. Madelyn bounced in the back, her teeth chattering because of the rough road. Then the movement stopped.

Cold fear cut all the way down her bones as she anticipated what might happen next.

* * *

Zach radioed Lynn at the office.

"Have you gotten up with Tyler yet?" He jumped straight to business.

"He said today was his day off. He was going to hang out with Thad."

His suspicions only rose. Tyler was definitely up to something. "If you hear from him, let me know."

"Will do. The mayor is still here, chief. Calls are flooding in. People have a lot of questions for you."

"I'll address all of them as soon as I figure a few things out. Stall as much as you can. Okay?"

"Of course." She paused. "Sir?"

"Yes?"

"One more thing. I thought you should know that someone reported an abandoned car on the side of Lankford Highway, only a couple of miles out of town."

"An abandoned car is the least of my concerns right now," Zach said.

"It's Madelyn's."

Alarm flooded him. "She wasn't with her vehicle?"

"No, sir."

Unease stirred inside him. "Thanks."

"While you're on the phone, the mayor would like to have a word with—"

He hung up, knowing he didn't have time to waste playing politics, and rushed down the road.

He stopped up in front of Levi Watson's house again. This time, he had evidence in hand.

The former chief started to close the door when he spotted Zach, but Zach jammed a foot over the threshold to stop him. When the man backed up, Zach stepped into the foyer. He needed a moment of privacy.

"I've got to find Tyler, Levi."

He narrowed his eyes. "Haven't you started enough trouble?"

Zach held up the heroin he had discovered. "Your nephew has been behind the drug trade in the area. Or did you already know that?"

The chief's eyes widened. "Not my nephew."

"Believe it or not, he's involved. Now I can't get in touch with him. Do you know where he might be?"

He shook his head, his guard remaining up. "No idea."

"I need you to think. Where might he go to have some time to himself?"

"I told you, I don't know." His face reddened.

He was getting angry, Zach realized. Levi knew something. Zach had to get through to him.

"Levi, someone's life is on the line. Things are going to get far worse for Tyler if I don't find him soon. It's better if I get ahold of him before someone else does. If the other drug dealers get to him first, they'll kill him. If the feds find him before I do, he won't even have a chance. Is there anywhere he might go?"

Levi pressed his lips together a moment before nodding with resignation. "There's an old family place seaside near Oyster. He could be there."

Madelyn had been shoved into a small fishing cottage, and Tyler tied her to a heavy wooden chair. As he jerked the rope around her wrists tighter, she glanced around, gathering her surroundings.

The cottage was ratty and old. It even smelled old. The wood floor had numerous holes in it, and no doubt all kinds of creatures lurked in the crawlspace beneath. Yellowed wallpaper with orange-and-brown flowers lined up in stripes covered the room. A matching orange couch with several rips rested against the opposite wall.

"Don't go anywhere." Tyler smiled.

As he exited to the back of the property, Madelyn jerked against the ropes holding her. It was no use. She wasn't getting out of her ties. Instead, she focused on the window across the house.

She saw Tyler walking outside. Water stretched in the background. Tyler was talking to someone, but she couldn't tell who. He was obviously working with someone.

Finally, the back door slammed closed again and footsteps sounded across the rickety floor. Tyler walked back into the room.

"How could you do this?" Madelyn asked.

"When we heard there was a reporter coming to town, we had to try and discourage you."

"So you followed me here in the white truck?" Why had he suspected her?

Tyler shrugged. "Something like that. Everyone in town knew you were coming. The last thing we wanted was to increase tourism in the town, so I tried to scare you off. You aren't easily scared."

"But an influx of visitors would help a lot of people and their businesses. Why wouldn't you want that?" she asked.

He stared at her a moment before chuckling and shaking her head. "Don't pretend to be naive."

"I'm not. I have no idea what you're talking about. I didn't come here to investigate you."

A second of doubt flickered in his gaze. "Sure."

"But I can reasonably assume that all along you were the one behind the attacks that have happened since I've been in Waterman's Reach. I can't believe someone who's supposed to have the public's trust would betray them like this."

Tyler continued to pace. He had some kind of stick in his hand, and he continually smacked it against his palm. He reminded Madelyn of an executioner just waiting for a signal to go.

"Everything was supposed to point back to Zach. To

cast him in a bad light. It was just a matter of time before everything came crashing down around him. Until he fell in love with you."

In love? If that had been the case at one time, it wasn't anymore. Madelyn had seen the look in Zach's eyes after he read the article. It was pure hatred.

"Everything already crashed down around Zach," Madelyn said. "He lost his job and his life back in Baltimore, all because of accusations that weren't true. So why did you target him? Why are you so obsessed with him?"

Tyler shook his head. "You have a lot of questions. I guess that makes you a good reporter."

"Apparently that made me a threat. Zach Davis, as well."

He smiled, a cold, heartless grin, and began pacing again. "Exactly. I knew who Zach was when he came into town. He was getting closer to finding answers, and I had to take care of him. Then you showed up, and I had two problems on my hands."

Madelyn tugged at her bound hands again. "These drugs you're producing are killing people. You use people. You have no regard for how your actions impact other people's lives."

Tyler shrugged, as if Madelyn's revelation didn't bother him in the least. "You should have just let it go. After someone tried to shoot you, I was sure you would hit the road. But you didn't, so we had to keep coming at you. Now we need to get rid of you. Don't worry. We have some evidence that will make it look like Zach is responsible for this as well. We would have just let you leave peacefully, but having Zach accused of your murder will be the icing on the cake."

Anger surged in her. Tyler was going to ruin Zach. Madelyn couldn't let that happen.

He twirled a toothpick between his teeth like he didn't have a care in the world. Disgust roiled in Madelyn's stomach. How could people be this twisted? Then again, maybe she had no room to talk. She'd been ready to deceive people to get what she wanted also. Thankfully, she'd realized the error of her ways before it was too late.

"Were you the one who snatched those oysters from me my first night here?" Madelyn asked, still trying to put all the pieces together and buy time in the process.

"That was all a big mistake," Tyler said. "Eva grabbed the wrong ones from down at Thad's. She grabbed the ones that had heroin hidden inside."

Madelyn's mouth dropped open. "That's how you're transporting drugs? Through the seafood that's funneled through your friend's seafood market?"

Tyler shrugged. "It's worked like a charm for the past several years. We can't let anything ruin it. Soon, I'll be able to escape to a nice little place in the Caribbean. The drug trade is quite profitable."

"You're not going to get away with this." Madelyn struggled against her binds, her chair rocking back and forth as her actions became more frantic.

Tyler pulled out a Glock. "I stopped by Zach's place today to grab this. It's not his police-issued gun, but it's good enough."

Her throat went dry. He'd thought all of this out. "How'd you get in?"

"I used to work for Mayor Alan. I helped him mange his real estate. I just happened to make copies of all the keys when I worked for him, so now I can come and go as I want."

"Zach just changed his locks, though." Madelyn clearly remembered him saying that.

Tyler frowned. "I always have a backup plan. My cousin just happens to work at the hardware store where Zach bought his lock. When Zach had an extra key made for the mayor, my friend made one more, just in case. The things people do for money…"

"Some people will even trade their self-worth."

"Now, enough talking." Tyler aimed his gun right at Madelyn's chest.

She braced herself for the inevitable pain that would follow and quickly began lifting up prayers.

TWENTY-THREE

Zach stopped well before Tyler's fishing cottage and continued the rest of the way on foot. He'd called the Coast Guard and state police for backup, but they were at least twenty minutes out thanks to two hikers who'd gotten lost in a nearby state park located on the water. He couldn't wait for them—there was no time to waste. He felt certain that Madelyn's life was in danger.

At the thought of something happening to Madelyn, his chest tightened. Despite their rocky relationship and everything that had transpired between them, he knew he cared about her. He was convinced that article that had been published about him was somehow a setup and that the same person who was framing Zach was also framing Madelyn. Madelyn may have been involved, but Zach couldn't help but think it wasn't willingly—at least not in the end.

He drew his gun and slowly approached the ramshackle building. Beyond the edge, he saw Tyler's police cruiser.

He was here.

Tyler must have taken that missing bullet from the scene, as well as planted someone on the docks who looked like Zach. He wanted to make him look guilty. Zach wouldn't have a chance to discover the heroin operation if he was in jail.

He pressed himself against the building and listened as voices drifted outside from the window. He strained to make out what they were saying. It was no use. They were too far away.

The sound of Madelyn screaming cut through the air. Zach knew he had to take action. Now.

He kicked the front door open and burst inside. Tyler stood with his gun drawn toward Madelyn. Blood drizzled from her lip and her head hung low, like she was on the verge of losing consciousness. Reacting on instinct, Zach fired.

The bullet hit Tyler's arm near his shoulder, and the gun flew from his hand. Tyler fell to the ground, gasping in pain.

"Zach, watch out!" Madelyn yelled from the chair where she was tied up. Her words sounded weak, strained, and her eyes looked glazed.

He looked down and saw Tyler reach for the gun. Zach fired a shot at the floor, purposefully missing, and Tyler instantly withdrew. Reaching down, Zach grabbed the gun.

Tyler looked up at Zach, his eyes dark and his expression seething.

Zach raised his gun. "Don't make me use this."

Tyler paused and sneered. "Because we both know you will." He nodded. "That's right. I know what happened in Baltimore."

"It's not easy making these decisions, Tyler. Not something I take lightly." He meant the words. Those choices were burdens, not something he'd wish on other people. Those choices caused him to lose sleep at night, to question himself, to question his career. But he knew that came with the territory of justice. He'd been entrusted to protect people. That required lethal action at times.

"Why are you targeting me and Madelyn?"

"I heard she was coming to town, and I couldn't risk her

ruining the good thing we had going here. Plus, everyone was hoping her article would bring more tourism to the area. More tourism meant more people, which meant our setup would be ruined. I couldn't let that happen. As soon as we heard she was coming, we tried to run her off, but it didn't work. Then you got involved."

"You escalated," Zach said.

"When we broke into her place, we saw the research on her computer. We realized your connection with the heroin we're delivering up to Baltimore. We figured we'd kill two birds with one stone." He grasped his shoulder, blood oozing out around his fingers.

"I thought you were better than this, Tyler."

Tyler's eyes lit with fire as he glared at Zach from the floor. "You don't know anything about me. I don't want to be stuck in go-nowhere town for the rest of my life."

"The blood of all of the people who've died under the influence of that heroin is on your hands. I've been trying to stop it from being distributed. I don't want to see any more innocent people die."

"It's not my responsibility how people use the drug!"

"What about Bobby Wilson?" Madelyn asked. "How did he tie in to all of this?"

"He was helping us distribute. But we found out he was stealing from us. He threatened to tell law enforcement what we were doing if we didn't give him more. Like we weren't paying him enough. We had no choice but to kill him."

Tyler moaned again, grasping his arm where the bullet had grazed him. He might have to go to the hospital, but he would be okay. Zach could have easily done more damage.

"Zach, watch out—" Madelyn started.

Just then, something slammed into Zach's head. Before he could right himself, a fist connected with his jaw. Then everything went black.

* * *

Madelyn pulled against her binds, desperately wanting to get away. Beside her, Zach was tied to another chair. His head drooped down to his chin. He hadn't regained consciousness yet.

"We've got to get out of here," Tyler said, suddenly looking antsy. "Knowing Zach, he has backup coming. I called in a false report about some lost hikers, but that will only keep everyone occupied for so long."

"We should just leave," Thad said. "Get out of the country before they can stop us."

"But what about our plans to make it look like he was the one behind this?"

"We don't have any time for that right now," Thad insisted. "We've gotta go."

Apparently, Thad was Tyler's best friend. He must have been the one who'd helped Tyler with some of the crimes. He was big and burly and didn't look like the type of person Madelyn would want to run into in a dark alley.

Dear Lord, please be with Zach. Help him to be okay. Help us to get out of this...somehow.

The possibilities seemed slim. Tyler and Thad had guns, while Zach and Madelyn were tied up and had no weapons.

She hoped Zach had backup on the way. They desperately needed help.

Thad and Tyler paced outside. Madelyn was aware of every moment that ticked by. It seemed to inch her closer to her death. Anxiety knotted in her back, her shoulders, her neck.

Madelyn had to think.

She tugged at the rope around her wrists again. Finally, it started to give a little. But what would she do even if she broke free from her binds? She couldn't carry Zach to safety.

Just then, Zach moaned beside her. Madelyn jerked her

head toward him and saw his eyes starting to open. His face scrunched in pain as consciousness reminded him of his injuries. He was going to have a whopper of a headache.

"Are you okay?" she asked, wishing she could reach out to him.

He winced again when he saw her. "I've been better."

"We have to get out of here somehow, Zach." He probably hated her, but they had to work together. Besides, he had come to help her. Even if Zach had just been doing his job. Did that mean there was any hope for forgiveness? She had to believe there was.

He glanced around the room, his eyes still narrowed with pain. "Any ideas how?"

"I wish. We're out-weaponed."

"And maybe out of time." He cringed again.

At that moment, Tyler and Thad stomped back inside. Thad jerked Zach to his feet, and Tyler grabbed Madelyn. His wound had been covered up, but a red splotch in the center of the white makeshift bandage made it clear he still needed help.

The men took them outside to where the bay raged. Whitecaps surfaced every several feet, and the water looked tumultuous.

Tied onto a dock among the marsh grass was a small rowboat.

"Don't do it, Tyler," Zach warned.

"Do what?" Madelyn hardly wanted to ask the question. She knew the answer would only frighten her.

"A couple was found adrift in a rowboat a few months ago," Zach said through clenched teeth. His gaze sent daggers through Tyler and Thad. "They'd gotten caught out in a storm. They didn't make it. If you don't know these waters, it can be dangerous."

Tyler smirked. "I thought it sounded like a great idea. We've already moved your car. We've planted some drugs in the trunk. When they find your dead bodies in the boat adrift at sea, all the pieces will fit together, and you'll look as guilty as sin."

"I wouldn't be so sure of that," Zach muttered.

"Don't worry. We'll be long gone before anyone figures out what really happened."

Before they could struggle, Tyler pulled out two rags and splashed something on them. In the next instant, the cloth went over Madelyn's mouth. Her head swirled. Then she lost consciousness.

When Zach regained consciousness, he and Madelyn were sitting in a boat set adrift in the…ocean, Zach realized. This wasn't one of the bays or rivers that surrounded the area. The water was too deep, land was nowhere to be seen, and the waves were too large.

These waters could be treacherous, and this boat wouldn't make it for long.

He glanced over at Madelyn. She lay lifelessly in the bow of the tiny, rickety rowboat. Otherwise she appeared unharmed—thank God. There was only a small cut on her forehead, and her lip was swollen.

Things could have been much worse. They could have ended with a bullet wound.

He leaned toward her and squeezed her arm, shaking her. "Madelyn, can you hear me?"

She opened her eyes, blinked several times and finally sat up straight. When she saw the water all around them, she gasped. Her fingers dug into the wooden slats of the boat as her face went pale.

Her shaking ceased for a moment when her gaze fell on him. "Zach, you're okay?"

He nodded. "I am."

"I was afraid we were going to…going to die." She shook

her head as if trying to drive away all her fearful thoughts. Then her eyes widened again and she looked around.

Zach followed her gaze. Water was all that was visible as far as the eye could see. It was enough to frighten the calmest of personalities.

"Where…?" Madelyn closed her eyes as reality washed over her. "What are we going to do?"

He reached across the boat and squeezed her hand, trying to ground her. The last thing they needed was to lose their cool. "We just have to hold out hope. Maybe another boat will see us."

The temperature had probably dropped ten degrees since earlier. A cold front was on the way. With cold fronts sometimes came storms. Madelyn already looked pale. How much could she handle?

"I'm sorry, Zach." Her gaze suddenly looked both intense and apologetic.

"It's okay."

"I didn't know things would turn out like this." Her voice sounded raw and honest.

"I know." And in his gut, Zach did know.

Madelyn blinked as if she hadn't heard correctly. "You do?"

"I should have known better, Madelyn. But I've been betrayed before. I thought the worst, and I'm sorry."

"You have no reason to be sorry. I was the one who came here under false pretenses. I had no idea. My editor painted you as such a monster. I don't know how I could have been so stupid."

"We all make mistakes."

Madelyn shook her head, disbelief in her gaze. "How could you be so forgiving?"

Zach had an easy answer to that. "I've known the need for forgiveness in my own life. I had a hard time forgiving myself after those two officers died. I questioned every decision I'd made up until that point. I know how important mercy is."

"I don't deserve it." She shook her head again, her guilt obvious.

"None of us do. But the good part is that God gives it anyway."

She spontaneously leaned toward him and planted a kiss on his cheek. "Thank you."

Warmth spread through him. He wished he could enjoy the moment more, but he had other more pressing things to think about. Like survival. He hoped there'd be time for more of this later. "Thank me after we get out of this alive."

Just as he said the words, waves rocked the boat again. Water dipped over the edges and pooled at their feet. The wind whipped up around them, sending a promise of danger with it. With every second, their chance of survival lessened.

"What are we going to do?" Madelyn clung to the edges of the boat, her knuckles white.

The tide continued to push them farther out into the ocean. Zach wished they had a paddle or something that could help them move. But all their efforts would be futile. The ocean was too strong.

Their best chance of getting through this was being rescued. Chris had said he was sending out a team after Zach called him earlier. But if Tyler figured out what he'd done, he would misdirect the Coast Guard. That's what he'd been doing all along, if Zach had to guess.

A bad feeling churned in his gut.

"Just hold on," Zach yelled, raising his voice to be heard over the wind.

More water sloshed into the boat as the ocean grumbled around them.

He looked behind him as Madelyn gasped. As he did, a huge wave washed over their boat and sent them both flying into the ocean.

TWENTY-FOUR

Cold water hit Madelyn's face. Covered her body. Submerged her.

The chill took her breath away.

She scrambled to find the surface, to find air for her lungs. But the current pulled her under and made it impossible to right herself or gain any control.

As another wave submerged her, strong arms surrounded her waist. The next instant, she broke the surface and gulped in air.

Zach, she realized. Zach had rescued her.

He was always there, always saving her.

"We're going to be okay," he assured her, one arm still holding her up while the other treaded water.

But how could he know how everything would turn out? Life didn't always work out the way we wanted.

Lord, help us now. Please.

After whispering *amen*, she searched in the distance for the rowboat. It was probably twenty feet away already. How had that happened so quickly?

"We need to get to the boat. It will give us something to hold on to. Can you make it?" Zach asked as a wave washed over them.

Madelyn sputtered a moment, fighting panic. Finally, she nodded, although she wasn't certain at all that she would make it. Her limbs already felt tired and spent. Battling the ocean waters had drained her.

She gave it everything she had and pushed herself through the water toward the boat. For every foot closer, the boat seemed to slip away an equal distance.

Zach paused beside her, treading water. Worry creased the corners of his eyes. "Can you wait here? I'll get the boat and bring it back."

Madelyn nodded, but her teeth were already beginning to chatter. She wasn't going to be able to do this much longer. "Okay."

Zach dove into the water. She held her breath, waiting for him to resurface. Finally, his head bobbed in the water several feet away.

Thank you, Jesus.

A few moments later, Zach pulled the boat back. Madelyn dragged herself halfway in. At least part of her body was out of the frigid water. But with every wave, with every second in the cold, her strength lessened.

"You can do this, Madelyn," Zach said, holding on to the boat beside her.

She tried to nod but wasn't sure if she succeeded.

"I'm here with you," he told her. "You're not alone."

Something about his words gripped her heart. She wasn't alone. Even after seeing the horrible way she'd acted, Zach had stuck with her. Rescued her. Maybe even loved her.

Just then a boat appeared in the distance.

Madelyn saw the Coast Guard emblem on the side.

They were safe. Finally, they were safe.

Chris wrapped blankets around both Zach and Madelyn as they huddled on plastic seats in the cabin of the boat. Hot air blared from a smaller heater in front of them.

Warmth had never felt so good.

"I'm glad we found you when we did," Chris said, sitting across from them. "I followed your lead, Zach, but I didn't see anyone at the cabin when I arrived. We decided to check the waterways."

"We've got to go after them," Madelyn said. Her teeth still chattered, and her hands shook so badly she couldn't hold any coffee.

Zach wished she would drink something warm, but at least they'd be on shore soon. Medics could check her out for hypothermia.

"I don't think you're in a state to go anywhere," Zach said.

She shook her head. Despite everything that had happened, determination still stained her gaze. "We don't have a choice. They're going to head to the Caribbean. I heard them talking about it."

"How do they plan on getting there?" Chris asked. "To traverse those waters, they'll need a bigger boat than any they can dock at the creek by their cabin."

"They won't waste any time leaving," Madelyn said, staring off into the distance for a moment. "We've got to go to the marina in Waterman's Reach. The boats there are the only ones big enough to be out in this weather and not be destroyed."

"We'll head there now," Chris said. He called instructions to the captain at the wheel in front of them.

Zach's mind raced. Finally Madelyn was safe. But he couldn't let Tyler and Thad get away with all of this. More people would just get hurt in the long run if they continued their drug running.

Madelyn pointed in the distance. "There's another boat crazy enough to be out in this weather. Do you think…?"

Zach stood, squinting as he tried to get a better look. "Chris, can we pull up closer?"

"You got it."

As they got closer to the boat, a familiar figure appeared on the deck.

Tyler.

He and Thad were a good half a mile away from the Waterman's Reach harbor and probably thinking they were home free.

Just then, a bullet shot through the air, piercing the glass near them. They were firing on them, Zach realized.

"Take cover!" Chris shouted.

Zach pulled Madelyn to the floor. Shouts sounded outside. More bullets were fired. Some of the coasties on board ran on the deck, taking cover and grabbing their own weapons.

"What are you guys doing?" Zach asked Chris as he tried to figure out their plan of action.

Chris glanced toward the window beyond him. "As soon as it's safe, my people will board and take them into custody. They're outnumbered, and we've got a bigger boat. There's no way they're getting away from us."

More gunshots sounded and more shouts roared outside the cabin. The boat tossed in the water, much more stable than the rowboat, but ocean right now still offered a rough ride.

"What's going on now?" Zach asked, desperate to look for himself. He tried to stay close to Madelyn, though. Her skin almost had a bluish tint to it that worried him.

Chris peered through the window. "My men are on board the yacht. They caught one guy. The burly one."

Thad, Zach realized. "What about Tyler?"

"They're still looking for him," Chris said.

"Stay here," Zach told Madelyn. "Please. I want to see what's going on out there myself."

She nodded.

Zach looked at his friend. "Chris, you have any objections?"

"You're an officer of the law. Proceed at your own risk."

Zach leaned toward Madelyn and brushed a kiss across her forehead. "I love you."

A smile spread across her lips. "I love you, too. I'll be fine. Now go get him."

Zach stepped onto the deck and peered over the rail. As a chilly wind hit him, he shivered. He ignored the cold and watched as coasties searched the yacht.

Where was Tyler? The man couldn't have gone but so far. His boat was a decent size, but it wasn't so big that he shouldn't have been discovered yet.

Just then, Zach spotted someone in the water, swimming away from the scene.

Tyler!

Zach glanced around. No one else appeared to have spotted him.

No way was he letting Tyler get away.

Without time to second-guess himself, he jumped into the water. Biting cold surrounded him, but he didn't care. He'd have time to get warm later.

Zach used every last ounce of his energy to propel himself through the water. He took big strokes, not giving himself time to think about the pain tingling at his fingertips and toes.

He quickly closed in on Tyler, who seemed to flail at the shock of the water. He was struggling to swim through the cold.

Finally, Zach was close enough to grab the man's shoulder. He dragged Tyler to a stop before raising his fist and punching him square on the face.

Tyler sputtered, struggling just to stay afloat.

"You didn't think you were going to get away with this, did you?" Zach asked.

Tyler moaned. "I did actually. I was so close."

Before Zach could respond, Coast Guard vessels surrounded them. They took Tyler into custody and pulled Zach out of the water.

It was over. It was finally all over.

EPILOGUE

Madelyn stood on the shores of the Chesapeake Bay and let the breeze wash over her. She gulped in a deep breath of fresh air. She could really get used to being here.

Despite everything that had happened, life had somehow worked out.

Tyler and Thad were captured as they'd tried to escape to Bermuda. Based on the staggering amount of evidence proving their involvement in the drug-trafficking ring in Waterman's Reach, it looked like they'd be spending a long time in jail.

Zach's reputation had been restored. In fact, a few national newspapers had run a story on his heroism. His name was finally free and clear, and several law enforcement agencies had contacted him about job opportunities. He could put everything that had happened behind him.

Madelyn had given up her job with East Coast International. When she'd gone in to the office to turn in her resignation, she'd been surprised to discover that Paula had been fired once people discovered she'd written that article on Zach and put Madelyn's name on it.

In a surprising turn of events, Madelyn had discovered that Paula and Mario, the boy killed in the drug bust, were actually cousins. Paula wanted revenge on Zach for her perceived injustice. She wasn't willing to come to Waterman's

Reach herself because she feared Zach would recognize her. Apparently, they'd had a confrontation at Mario's funeral.

She wanted to put that part of her past behind her. Her drive to succeed had made her compromise her convictions. She couldn't let that happen again. Instead, she would free-lance for some local magazines for a while until she figured out what kind of permanent, full-time job she wanted.

And, last but not least, Waterman's Reach was getting the boost the town had hoped for. With all of the media attention, the town had practically been made famous. People were coming out to see the place that time left behind. Even Eva and Milton seemed to have forgiven Madelyn for the misunderstanding, and both had been cleared of any involvement.

Someone appeared behind her on the shore and wrapped his arms around her waist. She grinned.

Zach.

"I thought I might find you out here," he said, his breath hitting her ear.

"This is my favorite place. Now I'm here with my favorite person. It doesn't get much better than this."

"It doesn't, does it?" He rested his chin on her shoulder.

Just being in his arms made her feel safe and secure, like she was stronger for it. It had been a hard journey to get here, but it felt good to finally have arrived.

"So, what did you decide?" She turned to face him.

Just seeing Zach's features made her feel warm and cherished. She wanted to memorize the lines of his face and the sound of his laughter and the feeling of being so close to him.

"I decided to stay," he said.

She raised her eyebrows. "You're staying in Waterman's Reach. I'm surprised."

"Disappointed?" he asked.

She shook her head. "No, not at all. It's a great little town."

"I agree. However, I won't be chief. I'm going to work for the state police."

"That's great."

He nodded. "I can finally build on that nice little piece of property. I can put down some roots."

She smiled. "It sounds like everything you've ever wanted. You deserve it, Zach."

"I'm hoping you might stick around with me."

Her heart sped up.

"I know we haven't known each other that long. Only a few months now. But I want to spend forever with you, Madelyn. I want us to make a life together."

"Are you serious?"

"More than ever." He got down on one knee. "Madelyn Sawyer, will you marry me?"

She stared at the ring in his hand before a huge smile spread across her face. "Yes. Yes, I will!"

He slipped the ring on her finger before standing and pulling her into a long embrace.

Madelyn could hardly believe she'd found love with the very man she was supposed to expose. After everything they'd been through, she'd never doubt him again. Zach had gone from being the story of a lifetime to being the love of her life.

And she couldn't be happier about it.

* * * * *

Dear Reader,

Thank you so much for taking the time to read *Dark Harbor*. I hope you enjoyed getting to know Zach Davis and Madelyn Sawyer just as much as I did.

While I wrote this book, I was able to spend a significant amount of time on Virginia's Eastern Shore, where this book takes place. I visited the small towns there and formulated ideas for the fictional town of Waterman's Reach. The Eastern Shore truly is a gem and, in so many ways, untouched. There's a quieter pace of life between the farmlands, the bay and the ocean.

In *Dark Harbor*, Zach Davis was held responsible for a crime he didn't commit. We can be thankful that Jesus paid for sins He didn't commit when He died on the cross in order to give us hope. No matter what's happened in our past or what's happening now in our lives, we can rest assured that God is watching over us, that He loves us and that He's got everything under control. God truly is a harbor for us all, in times of storms and peace.

Many blessings,
Christy Barritt

COMING NEXT MONTH FROM
Love Inspired® Suspense

Available July 5, 2016

HONOR AND DEFEND
Rookie K-9 Unit • by Lynette Eason
Fresh out of prison after being framed for a robbery, Lee Earnshaw learns the police have no leads in the investigation into his sister's murder. So he teams up with his former love, K-9 officer Ellen Foxcroft, and her golden retriever partner to catch the killer.

DANGEROUS LEGACY • by Valerie Hansen
When Flint Crawford returns to his Arkansas hometown, he's greeted by old love Maggie Morgan—and flying bullets. Has their old family feud escalated to the point that someone close wants them dead before they have a chance to renew their love?

IN A KILLER'S SIGHTS
Smoky Mountain Secrets • by Sandra Robbins
After Dean Harwell witnesses someone attacking his ex-wife near his ranch, the former cop promises to protect her. But will he stay by Gwen's side once he learns about the secret she's kept hidden from him?

BLINDSIDED
Roads to Danger • by Katy Lee
Undercover FBI agent Ethan Gunn's goal is to take down a human trafficking ring...until they kidnap racetrack owner Roni Spencer. Now he'll risk anything—including his cover and the investigation—to rescue her.

INCRIMINATING EVIDENCE • by Rachel Dylan
Fighting to bring an organized crime syndicate to justice, rookie prosecutor Jessica Hughes is assigned handsome rookie FBI agent Zach Taylor as her protector. But the closer they get to the criminals—and each other—the more dangerous both their jobs become.

FRACTURED MEMORY • by Jordyn Redwood
Julia Galloway escaped a serial killer with her life but not her memory. Now, as someone tries to finish the killer's work, she must rely on US marshal Eli Cayne—a man with whom she shares a past she can't remember—to keep her safe.

LOOK FOR THESE AND OTHER LOVE INSPIRED BOOKS WHEREVER BOOKS ARE SOLD, INCLUDING MOST BOOKSTORES, SUPERMARKETS, DISCOUNT STORES AND DRUGSTORES.

LISCNM0616

REQUEST YOUR FREE BOOKS!
2 FREE RIVETING INSPIRATIONAL NOVELS
PLUS 2 FREE MYSTERY GIFTS

Love Inspired.
SUSPENSE
RIVETING INSPIRATIONAL ROMANCE

YES! Please send me 2 FREE Love Inspired® Suspense novels and my 2 FREE mystery gifts (gifts are worth about $10). After receiving them, if I don't wish to receive any more books, I can return the shipping statement marked "cancel." If I don't cancel, I will receive 4 brand-new novels every month and be billed just $4.99 per book in the U.S. or $5.49 per book in Canada. That's a savings of at least 17% off the cover price. It's quite a bargain! Shipping and handling is just 50¢ per book in the U.S. and 75¢ per book in Canada.* I understand that accepting the 2 free books and gifts places me under no obligation to buy anything. I can always return a shipment and cancel at any time. Even if I never buy another book, the two free books and gifts are mine to keep forever.

123/323 IDN GH5Z

Name	(PLEASE PRINT)
Address	Apt. #
City	State/Prov.	Zip/Postal Code

Signature (if under 18, a parent or guardian must sign)

Mail to the **Reader Service:**
IN U.S.A.: P.O. Box 1867, Buffalo, NY 14240-1867
IN CANADA: P.O. Box 609, Fort Erie, Ontario L2A 5X3

**Are you a current subscriber to Love Inspired® Suspense books
and want to receive the larger-print edition?
Call 1-800-873-8635 or visit www.ReaderService.com.**

* Terms and prices subject to change without notice. Prices do not include applicable taxes. Sales tax applicable in N.Y. Canadian residents will be charged applicable taxes. Offer not valid in Quebec. This offer is limited to one order per household. Not valid for current subscribers to Love Inspired Suspense books. All orders subject to credit approval. Credit or debit balances in a customer's account(s) may be offset by any other outstanding balance owed by or to the customer. Please allow 4 to 6 weeks for delivery. Offer available while quantities last.

Your Privacy—The Reader Service is committed to protecting your privacy. Our Privacy Policy is available online at www.ReaderService.com or upon request from the Reader Service.

We make a portion of our mailing list available to reputable third parties that offer products we believe may interest you. If you prefer that we not exchange your name with third parties, or if you wish to clarify or modify your communication preferences, please visit us at www.ReaderService.com/consumerschoice or write to us at Reader Service Preference Service, P.O. Box 9062, Buffalo, NY 14240-9062. Include your complete name and address.

LIS15

SPECIAL EXCERPT FROM

Love Inspired
SUSPENSE

A rookie K-9 officer must work together with her former love to stay alive and solve the mystery of his sister's murder.

Read on for an excerpt from
HONOR AND DEFEND,
the next book in the exciting K-9 cop miniseries
ROOKIE K-9 UNIT.

K-9 police officer Ellen Foxcroft shot a sideways glance at the man who drove in silent concentration. Just ten minutes ago, they'd picked up three puppies from Sophie Williams. Not only was she a trainer for the Desert Valley K-9 training center, she also worked with the Prison Pups program. A program Lee Earnshaw, the man behind the wheel, was intimately familiar with since he'd worked with the program up until two weeks ago, when he'd been released from prison. Framed. Set up by a dirty cop, he'd lost two years of his life.

"I appreciate you giving me this chance to work with you and the pups. Not everyone believes I'm innocent in spite of the press conference and Ken Bucks's arrest," Lee said.

"You're welcome."

"I just really want to put it all behind me."

"I'm sure you do." Probably easier said than done. This was Lee's second day on the job. Two days ago, after much self-examination and encouragement from Sophie, she'd approached Lee about working for her and he'd been reluctant. With their history, she couldn't say she blamed him. They'd dated in high school. Until she'd allowed her mother to chase him away. Her jaw tightened. She didn't want to go there.

Instead, she remembered the flare of attraction she'd felt just from being in his presence again. Just from talking to him and looking into his eyes. Eyes she'd never been able to forget.

She couldn't help studying his features. Brown hair with a brand-new cut, brown eyes that at times looked hard and cold but were always alive and warm when he worked with the animals. His strong jaw held a five-o'clock shadow.

"I can understand your frustrations, Lee. I feel the same way—"

The back windshield shattered and Ellen gave a low scream of surprise. Lee jerked the wheel to the right. "Get down!" Outside sounds rushed through the missing window. Someone was shooting at them!

Don't miss HONOR AND DEFEND
by Lynette Eason, available wherever
Love Inspired® Suspense books and ebooks are sold.

www.LoveInspired.com

Reading Has Its Rewards

Earn **FREE BOOKS!**

Register at **Harlequin My Rewards** and submit your Harlequin purchases from wherever you shop to earn points for free books and other exclusive rewards.

Plus submit your purchases from now till May 30th for a chance to win a $500 Visa Card*.

Visit **HarlequinMyRewards.com** today

Earn **FREE REWARDS** Join Today! HarlequinMyRewards.com

MYRI6RI